THE GLUT

MATTHEW CASH

BURDIZZO BOOKS

2022

Chapter 1

Fighting for breath, Vince clutches handfuls of sweat-soaked bed sheets as he tries to pull all thirty-two stones of himself into an upright position. He rolls onto his left side, his arm instantly going numb, and pushes himself into a sitting position. His heart thuds, his head droops over his chest. *Sleep apnoea*. It happens at least six times a night, yet he still hasn't told the doctors at the weight-loss clinic.

Beside the bed, a dozen chocolate wrappers; the taste still on his tongue, and the fear of yet another ailment caused by his obesity only makes him want more.

"...discovery is phenomenal, first of its kind ever in our lifetime, that's for sure, Patrick..."

Vince switches off the radio and pounds his fists at the tummy fat that sits across his thighs, at the huge heavy sacks of flesh that hang above it. His tits. The tits that the school bullies would grab and poke, poke and grab and leave finger-marked bruises on when they had him up against the lockers outside the science labs.

Haha, Vince has got bigger boobs than Michelle Docker.

Vince grabs them and wishes he had the power to tear off the unsightly blubber and throw it away.

No matter how many times it happens, no matter how many years of it, the looks *still* hurt. Vince attracts attention wherever he goes, from subtle double-takes to outright disgusted glares. Even the politest of people will mutter under their breath to one another about his size. Others shout coarse and offensive things, as though his size cushions him from such abuse.

There is no positivity in his life; Vince has lost count of the number of nutritional plans and diets he has tried, the different physicians who have tried to help, scare and force him into losing weight. He is a seasoned veteran when it comes to diets, knows exactly how they work, what to do, everything, but knows that none of them are any use unless you have the motivation and willpower. He has neither and he can't stop eating.

He eats when he is happy.

He eats when he is sad.

He eats when he is angry.

He eats when he is bored.

Almost every strong emotion is a reason to gorge himself.

"You realise that this is just a slow and lingering death, don't you?" the physician says, matter-of-factly.

"Yeah, I know." Vince feels familiar tears at the harsh words, words he has heard thousands of times — the earliest when he was seven years old and a general practitioner told him he would be dead by the time he was twelve if he didn't lose weight.

"Your joints can't support your weight."

Vince grips the metal crutches, nods.

"You've put on another stone since your last visit four weeks ago."

"I can't help it." The tears flow freely and he averts his eyes from the stick-thin doctor.

"But you can, Vincent, we've been through this time and time again. You can do it."

Vince begins to shake his head but stops as he knows it will infuriate the doctor even more.

"Willpower and self-belief." He makes it sound so easy, but it isn't easy at all, not for him.

Vince leaves the doctor's office and walks past the waiting patients with their sympathetic stares. He is the heaviest at the clinic now Henry has left.

Vince scowls at the thought of him. Henry Green had become the local celebrity a year or so ago due to his dramatic weight loss: fifteen stones.

Vince had devoured all the articles in the papers, hoping to discover the secret of Henry's unshakeable willpower but there was little more than the usual generic crap about mind-over-matter. He'd seen the weight fall off that man like it was nothing, but more importantly, he remembered the filthy, dishevelled, pessimistic thing he had been before.

Henry Green had been a thirty-stone mountain covered in a mass of black hair and beard.

He had taken no pride in his appearance or personal hygiene and had clearly given up on life, yet one day he had come into the clinic with an ecstatic look on his face and announced he was going to beat his obesity. And sure enough, with every passing month, he would come in a stone or more lighter.

Vince wants to know exactly what it was that Henry suddenly changed. He has watched no end of inspirational videos of miraculous weight-loss victories and whilst there is a spark of that belief during the duration of the videos, it never burns for long before he is quenched by the same old dampening self-doubt.

He needs to know Henry's secret: how, in the space of two years, he has gone from a lonely, thirty-stone tramp to a chiselled Adonis who dates women half his age.

Chapter 2

Vince knows where Henry lives but has never visited. He waits for what feels like hours for Henry's current squeeze to leave before walking across to his ground floor flat. Anger and jealousy fill him as Henry darts out, wearing only jeans and a t-shirt, and puts two paper takeaway sacks in the recycling bin.

"Oi," Vince calls, waving one of his sticks.

Henry clocks him and Vince sees his pained expression. He knows that look. "Oh, hey, it's Vince, isn't it?"

"Yeah," Vince says, shuffling up to him.

Henry has one hand on his open front door, eager to be inside. "Good to see you."

Vince puts a hand on the door to stop him from closing it. "You're looking well, Henry."

Once again with the sympathy, "Thanks, Vince. Umm, are you still going to the clinic?"

Vince nods and is delighted by how Henry tries to squirm his way inside. There is no loose skin anywhere, even on his triceps. He must have had surgery.

Henry's pained expression worsens when he feels Vince scrutinising him. "Well, I best be getting in."

"Tell me how you did it, Henry, tell me!" Vince snaps, and pushes himself further into the doorway.

"Look man, you read the articles," Henry says, trying to close the door.

"That was all generic bollocks, I know how you were, I remember how you used to think."

Henry's smile is as uncomfortable as they come. "Look, I had one of those, *what-do-you-call-its*, epiphanies." He pauses and looks solemnly into Vince's eyes. "You can do it too, you know."

Vince feels himself bubble with anger and prays that Henry isn't about to follow up with —

"I believe in you, bro."

Damn.

Vince slams into the half-open door, barrelling into Henry and sending him reeling into the hallway of his flat. The floor is littered with takeaway flyers and empty pizza boxes. The smell of greasy fried food permeates the place. Boxes of unopened chocolate bars are stacked from floor to ceiling. Vince grabs Henry around the throat and thrusts him against the wall. "What the fuck is your secret?"

"There's no secret, I promise, only willpower," Henry whines.

"I don't believe you!" Vince shakes the man. "Is it an illegal diet drug? What?" His anger soon dissipates into begging sorrow and he half-collapses against Henry.

"Jesus, Vince, man, you're crushing me."

Vince straightens up and lets him go; the exertion having taken its toll, he fights for breath. "Please, Henry."

"*Daddy.*"

Both men turn towards a voice coming from the bedroom's closed door.

"I didn't know you had children," Vince says, before realising the voice sounded like a grown-up's. He moves away from Henry and walks towards the door.

"Fine, I'll tell you, okay?" Henry sighs, grabbing Vince by the forearm and pulling him away from the bedroom door. "But not here. Meet me at The Triffid later, say eight?"

"What?" Vince begins, but the sudden rush of happiness he feels at the prospect of finally getting answers, coupled with Henry's sudden increase in strength, makes him stop talking and he allows himself to be led out of the flat.

Chapter 3

Vince can't resist the allure of the takeaways as he walks away from Henry's flat and before he passes the second one, he is inside and perusing the badly-spelled menu. A television is playing a news report, something about space. He can't hear what they're saying as there's music playing over it but a headline says something about a comet. *Hopefully it'll fucking hit us*, Vince thinks, and looks at the two guys behind the counter. They smirk at each other.

"Oh, I bet you're just fucking thinking of the pound signs, aren't you?"

"What can I get you, sir?" says one of the men, avoiding eye contact.

"Oh, how about a fucking salad?" Vince is still pissed off but his eyes light up upon spotting an appetising item on the menu. "Give me the sixteen-inch *Vaggie Dulux,* please." Vince smirks triumphantly, even though the two men don't understand he is mocking them and their atrocious spelling. "I hope the *vaggies* are fresh!"

"Yes, we only use fresh vag." The man barks off orders to his colleague in his native language and they go about preparing Vince's order.

Vince eases himself onto a seat by the window to wait for his food and wonders about Henry's secret. It must be especially hard living so close to a street full of fast-food outlets.

Oh, God, I hope it's not a self-help program. Where weight loss and dieting are concerned, Vince has done it all, and listening to patronising knobheads talk about mind-over-matter and positive thinking makes him want to bury his face in a Black Forest gateau.

Listen to these relaxing forest sounds and forget everything about bingeing.

De-stress amongst nature.

It is bollocks.

Everything makes him think about food.

Everything.

Unless Henry's secret is an injection of willpower via a transorbital needle directly into his brain, it isn't going to work. But still, Henry Green has done the unthinkable. He has gone from being the fattest, most depressive person Vince has ever met, to someone who looks like they have never even heard the words 'eating disorder'.

"Your Vaggie Dulux."

Vince walks home with his Vaggie Dulux and a heavy, pessimistic heart. He really does hope a comet will come and put him out of his misery, but only after he's eaten his pizza.

Chapter 4

"Alright, Big 'un?"

Vince feels himself swallow the familiar embarrassment as he lets the complete stranger pass, and enters The Triffid.

How can people think it's alright to greet strangers that way?

Would they greet someone in a wheelchair with, 'Alright, Wheelie?'

A blind person with, 'Wotcha, Stevie?'

For fuck's sake.

Vince asks for a diet coke, ignores the barmaid's snigger, and goes to sit at the most inconspicuous table in the pub.

Henry is a quarter-of-an-hour late. When he eventually arrives, the dreary patrons light up as though a celebrity has walked in. A chorus of *'Oi, oi Greenie'* comes from a group of lads crowded around a fruit machine and the barmaid readjusts her tits and checks her makeup in the mirror behind the optics.

Fuck's sake.

Henry wears skinny-fit black jeans and a matching t-shirt which shows off a tight, muscular physique. The only way Vince can identify him is his face. This isn't just post-obese Henry Green, this is a Henry Green from the multiverse, from a dimension where he has never been so much as an ounce overweight in his life, where he actively joined sports teams after school as a child and grew up to be a personal trainer.

Vince watches him order a tall glass of sparkling mineral water and flash the barmaid a smile that no doubt moistens her knickers. He catches his eye with a grimace and makes his way across the bar.

Henry sits down opposite Vince and smiles awkwardly.

"Didn't think you were coming."

"I said I was, didn't I?"

"Why is this so hard for you to share?" Vince is even more certain that however Henry has undergone this fantastic metamorphosis, it can't have been legal.

Henry sips his drink and continues to avoid eye contact.

"It's drugs, isn't it?" Vince whispers, leaning over the table. "Look, man, at this fucking stage in my life I don't even care. I'll do anything. I can't live like this anymore. I'd rather die trying."

When Henry meets his eyes, Vince can see the onset of tears. "There's no going back once you've started."

I knew it. Vince takes a deep breath and lets it out slowly. Henry has practically confirmed it. "I don't care. I've got money. I'll do anything. How much?"

Henry gives a bitter laugh which reminds Vince of the pessimistic twat he used to be. "It doesn't cost a lot. Not in money, anyway."

"What, then? Just fucking tell me, for fuck's sake!"

Henry tells him.

Chapter 5

Vince squeezes the screwed-up ball of paper in his hoodie pocket and swears for the twenty-fourth time since leaving The Triffid.

The fucking wanker. The fucking evil, fucking wanker.

He hasn't hit anyone since high school but once Henry reveals the apparent secret to his success, he lashes out and strikes him with a left hook to the cheek. The group of lads from the fruit machine are on him in seconds, three grabbing him whilst another helps Henry up off the floor. Henry tells them everything's okay, to leave it, they listen and let him go.

"It's true, Vince. It's fucking true," Henry spits, raising a hand to his rapidly swelling eye.

"It's fucking bollocks is what it is."

"Try it, then," Henry retorts. "You've got nothing to lose." He pauses and points at Vince's belly. "Apart from that."

It is bollocks.

It has to be.

Complete and utter bollocks.

The anger swells up inside him all the way home, elevating his heart rate and making him drip with sweat.

Vince slams the door shut, yanks off his hoodie, and goes straight for the kitchen. His crutches fall to the floor and he hits the cupboards, a junkie searching for a hidden stash. Everything goes into his mouth without any hesitation as he tears open packets and cartons to find the Holy Grail.

Wrappers and tins are discarded where they fall, his mouth working furiously at biscuits, crisps, and canned custard purely for lubrication. His eyes widen when he finds what he is looking for and he falls to his aching knees and reaches for the Cadbury's purple. It is the biggest bar you can buy and he goes at it like a woodchipper, cramming as much into his mouth as possible and eating as fast as he can. No matter how big the bar of chocolate, he won't be satisfied until it is all gone. A frantic wheezing with porcine grunts fills the kitchen but Vince doesn't notice the noises he makes. All that matters is gorging himself, suffocating the pain inside him and burying it in food.

When all the chocolate is gone, he falls back against the cooker and howls a silent scream, thick with gloopy strings of chocolate-laced saliva.

All hope has gone, Henry is a raving lunatic, and Vince knows he will die like this.

.

The Glut

Chapter 6

Vince secretly refers to his demon as *Mr Hide*, an intentional play on Dr Jekyll's alter ego. Mr Hide takes over when hunger strikes; he lives inside Vince's stomach but has tentacles which poke and probe, and he has the ability to temporarily control his brain. At least that's what it feels like when he is ransacking cupboards for junk food or, if he is on one of his health fads, booking a taxi to take him to the supermarket at stupid o'clock when he can't cope with the lack of junk food at home. It's as if someone else is in the driver's seat, another personality that takes over and just wants to feed, feed, feed, and Vince is powerless, a backseat rider who can only sit back and watch as this beast destroys his body. Mr Hide always returns, more resilient than ever, and he always retreats into his soft, warm nest when the guilt and remorse and downright disgust set in afterwards.

Mr Hide only ever takes.

Vince sees him as the demon of gluttony; he can infect addicts of any vice, dipping his greasy fingers into the minds of the weak and forcing them to quit. These are his own personal feelings towards that part of him, and he knows, *really knows*, that it is himself doing it, it's him that makes him eat to excess, and when Henry started prattling on about something quite literal, he naturally went apeshit.

There is no way he is going to believe there really is an actual demonic entity inside him, forcing him to eat.

Chapter 7

"You're not going to believe this," Henry had said, and he was right: Vince didn't believe it from the first sentence.

"There's a part of the human psyche, the part that craves, that's not supposed to be there, it's alien, a foreign entity."

Vince had kept quiet, despite his immediate inklings that Henry was about to spout off with some David Icke-level bullshit. He was surprised he didn't involve the fucking comet that was due to make pretty in the skies over the next few months.

Henry avoided looking at him again, ran his hand over his shaven jaw and laughed, possibly at the absurdity of what he had just said. "It's true, though." Henry seemed to be trying to convince himself. "This shit goes back to the Beginning. When God created Man, man."

Vince sighed, "Mate, what the fuck are you on about? Are you trying to tell me you lost all this weight and shit through some new-age meditation malarkey?"

Henry shook his head. "No, if only that shite worked. I guess it does, for some. But I was a pessimistic cunt." His eyes locked onto Vince's. "You remember what I was like, I thought, no, I *knew,* I was going to die some forty-stone whale."

"So, what the fuck did you do?" Vince demanded.

Henry sat back in his chair, folded his arms across his chest and smirked like a madman. "I fucking sold my soul."

"Oh for fuck's sake!" Vince slapped the table and looked away in annoyance.

"It's true. There's a ritual, a specific ritual to rid yourself of the part of you that craves stuff, but it comes at a cost."

"You think this is fucking funny?" Vince slammed his hand against the table again and gathered his crutches, ready to leave. "My fucking joints can't hold my weight. I could keel over any fucking moment. I. Can't. Stop. Eating. And you sit there blabbering about selling your fucking soul to Satan like a fucking nutter. It's not fucking funny. I'm dying here. Slowly eating myself to death. I'm suffocating beneath layers of fat and all you can do is take the piss."

Henry got to his feet and pushed a folded square of paper across the table. "You know the stuff I was into." He motioned to the black symbols tattooed on his arms. "All this means something to me, you know."

"I just thought you were a fat heavy metal fan, not a fucking devil worshipper!" With the aid of his crutches, Vince forced himself to his feet.

"Well at least I believed in something aside from just stuffing my fucking face!"

And that was when Vince had hit him. It wasn't the slur that hurt as such, it was more the fact that it had come from someone who, a few years ago, was even heavier than he was.

The Glut

Chapter 8

Vince drags his hoodie across the litter-strewn kitchen floor and takes out Henry's screwed-up offering; even though he had pocketed it, he hasn't given it a single glance until now.

It is an A3 photocopy of two pages from a book, the title headers are blacked out with ink. In italics, it tells Vince that the following ritual is for summoning and separating an entity called *The Glut*.

Beneath a paragraph detailing what little knowledge the author has about this demonic being, which Vince glosses over at first, is a drawing of the grossest thing he has ever seen.

The thing is vaguely humanoid but grossly fat. A colossal, extended stomach hangs in a sack over legs that are either non-existent or hidden. Gaping splits run up its bulging sides and bubbling fat and seepage is depicted in graphic detail. Four giant, doughy arms protrude from this blubbersome torso, each roll of fat has filth and grease oozing from between the folds. Four hands are held out, palms downward, fingers dipping as though they are about to choose from an endless selection of hedonistic delicacies.

It is horrific. The face is the worst part, a vaguely spherical mass, completely hairless, rippling with endless, grime-coated chins. Tiny piggish eyes are barely visible over a mouth that seems to occupy the whole page. There is nothing humanoid about the mouth, it is just an orifice, a lipless vortex designed purely for consumption, endless consumption. All kinds of teeth, tusks, mandibles, anything that is designed to crush, mush and chew.

Making the beast look completely ridiculous is a single hook-shaped horn that hangs down parallel to its mouth like a wireless headset. Vince squints at the picture and sees a man skewered to the point. Either the man is outrageously small, or this demon really is gigantic.

Kaiju gigantic.

"How the fuck can Henry believe this shit?" Vince whispers and tries to read the words on the page. Most of the language is archaic but thankfully someone, he guesses Henry, has handwritten a translation around and beneath the hideous picture.

The Glut is in us all.

Every single one of us.

It lives inside us from the moment we are conceived.

It is Greed's original form.

Some of us are strong-willed, can resist its hold over us, but it will always be there unless severed. To cast it out is virtually irreversible but not impossible. Every addiction is borne from The Glut, that part inside you which feeds on your needs and grows stronger with each failure.

Alcoholics, drug addicts, pyromaniacs, sexual deviants, binge-eaters, kleptomaniacs.

The list is endless.

That little voice inside us that convinces us to do that thing one more time or have just one more hit of that magic stuff, that's The Glut.

It's got us wrapped beneath its stinking, sweat-stained arms, we're all touched by it but not all of us are able to control its influences.

This is how to separate yourself from The Glut.

How to free yourself from its grasp – forever.

It is the biggest load of bollocks Vince has ever read, but as with even the worst conspiracy theories a small voice inside him somewhere mutters *'What if?'*

Below Henry's sales talk are the instructions, detailing the way in which to perform the ritual, and that is more berserk than everything else on the page.

Vince's frustration and anger swiftly turn into self-hatred and pity. He will never get out of this fix he is in, never.

Letting the photocopied page flutter to the floor, he howls mournfully.

Chapter 9

After he can cry no more, Vince attempts the Herculean task of getting himself up off the floor. His worst nightmare, although he knows it is the inevitable destination his particular path is leading to, is being stuck for days until someone finds him, the fire brigade having to get him back on his feet.

He rolls over onto his hands and knees, and for a worrying second, he feels the strain in his wrists and knees. Images of his joints exploding in a red fury of white splinters makes him tremble but he manages to haul himself up.

He leans against the kitchen counter, and for the first time, considers suicide in a more rapid form than overeating.

Henry's page beckons out to him from the junk on the floor.

If only there were proof that it wasn't all shite.

He thinks about Henry's transformation, which, although miraculous, is still possible within the boundaries of science and the natural world.

He catches the first two instructions of the ritual preparations.

Do not wash, cut, shave, or clean any part of your body for six weeks.

{Even after toilet trips.}

After the six-week period remove and collect all bodily hair.

{All of it.}

That may explain why Henry had been such a dirty, smelly bastard when he turned up at the clinic.

People would move away when he entered the room; he hated that he fitted the *all fat people smell* stereotype.

He had always been a big hairy bastard, like an obese Rasputin, but Vince had put that down to the heavy metal scene. But just before he went off-radar and came back a stone lighter, he got really, really rancid. You could tell he was trying to mask the smell with copious amounts of deodorant and aftershave but it didn't work and you could see the filth and grime on him. It was foul.

And then, when he came back after missing a clinic, he was completely bald, clean-shaven, a stone lighter, and smelling fresh.

"Shiiit." Vince is starting to convince himself that it might actually work. He uses his litter grabber to pick the paper up off the floor and read the rest of the ritual preparations.

There is nothing that can cause him any permanent damage and he has never been vain where any part of his body is concerned; he is used to being disgusting.

Maybe this is a perverse kind of faith-healing?

If I can make myself have the willpower to do such degrading, gross things, maybe it will kick-start my willpower and show me that I'm capable of controlling my own body and mind, and the mythical Mr Hide, or Henry's Glut, will lose all potential hold over me.

What the fuck do I have to lose?

Chapter 10

The first week is easy enough. Staying in is easy for someone who doesn't go out much in the first place. The worst thing about it is the lack of hygiene after going to the toilet. By the end of the second day, a thick layer of crusted shit has matted the hair of his buttocks together like the strongest of Velcro.

When he goes to the toilet, he has to tear his arse cheeks apart with his hands, ripping out the dried faeces-covered hairs by the roots.

His crotch starts smelling strongly of kidneys and rotten fish.

It is not pleasant.

Not being able to wash his hands is horrible, but due to the paranoia borne in the Covid pandemic, he has boxes and boxes of latex gloves everywhere. There is nothing in Henry's list of rules to say he can't wear them when preparing or eating food. Although, after the fourth day, when he wakes up in the middle of the night to find the fingers of his right hand scrabbling away inside the hot, crusty-edged, crevice of his sopping wet arsehole, he considers wearing them twenty-four-seven.

Somehow, he manages to get through six weeks of this. He itches all over, has chronic toothache, has put on weight from even less activity than usual, has the worst case of bumfluff on his face he ever thought imaginable, and has some kind of white stuff growing in some of his deeper, moist areas. But he follows the ritual preparations, however disgusting they are, to the letter.

Chapter 11

Vince's stomach has grown stronger over the last six weeks and when he opens the plastic box he doesn't retch.

The third preparation had been another vile one.

Save all bodily excretions.

Henry made a detailed list in case any were left out.

Broken finger/toenails

Dandruff

Snot/saliva

Sweat {wring garments out}

Urine

Faeces

Sperm

Blood

Vomit

Followed by the cursory piece of advice:

TRY TO KEEP THEM SEPARATE.

Vince leans over the bath, removes the lid from the sixteen-litre box, lifts the tub, and tries his best not to look at it too long. He has his vomit bucket next to him just in case.

Inside the box is six weeks' worth of assorted faeces, from huge, impressively long logs that Vince can't help but feel a small ounce of paternal pride for, to putrid splatters that don't seem to have been passed by anything remotely human.

He takes a wallpaper scraper and begins to ease the dried korma stains from the sides of the box. A waft of stale shit puffs up around his face as he upends the contents into the bathtub. It is too much.

He quickly unscrews the lid of his vomit bucket and tops up the soupy orange mixture that is already in there with something that resembles pink scrambled eggs but smells like fish, cheese, and cinnamon.

"Oh, Jesus," he says, not bothering to wipe his mouth. He looks at the list of preparations and is thankful he can empty the vomit buckets.

He unscrews the lid of the first bucket and immediately adds more slop to the second. It has matured like a not-so-fine wine. He pours the peachy slosh on top of the shit and adds the second, dry-heaving all the way through the process.

The urine part takes the piss.

Three-dozen bottles to be exact. Vince never realised he drank so much.

He covers his mouth and nose with his sleeve and empties bottle after bottle of the stinking orange juice into the bath.

Luckily, Vince's deposit of sweat only fills a litre tub, but it still reeks when he opens it.

He has collected nail clippings, and anything that came off him whilst scratching, in empty herb jars — which he sprinkles over the unholy stew.

A matchbox holds the choicest of offerings from his nose: great, lengthy dangling things that have crisped and resemble pork rinds with added nasal hair.

It all goes in along with a small vial of blood from the time he accidentally cut himself on a can of salmon, and a half-filled hand sanitiser bottle of semen from when he had eight consecutive wanks over the space of three-and-a-half days about Nicki Minaj and Ru Paul.

Vince reads the next part several times to make sure he gets it right, understands the procedure. Henry hasn't interpreted the original spelling of the section title, but he has neatly crossed out what Vince guesses was Old English and updated.

Bodily Scraypinges

Chapter 12

Vince uses a butter knife; this way he knows he won't cut himself. He scrapes the blade across the skin of his forehead and is disgusted to see a collection of what looks like parmesan dotted with little black speckles of black pepper slough up on the knife blade.

He repeats this process over his whole face and neck, digging the tip of the knife inside the folds of his ears to gather thick, icky orange stuff the colour and consistency of melted cheese puffs.

The scabby tops of crusted-over blackheads and spots line up on the blade along with a rich, slightly translucent jus made from various different kinds of pus.

When he is finished with his face, he spreads the ghastly mixture on the side of the bath and strips off.

The stuff that comes off his arms and body is disgusting: thick, grey rancid shit, like rotten goose fat. It reminds him of a really weird film he once watched about this ratty-looking boy who had the world's most super-amazing nose or something. It was set in France and he was a right weirdo, could smell you from two miles away, and he started killing women to try and make a perfume from their scent. At one point in the movie he covered this woman in animal fat and tried to distil it to capture her smell. When Vince scrapes the filth off his body it is the same as when Nose-boy scrapes the fat off the lady's skin.

He pushes a teaspoon as deep as he can into his cavernous belly button, twists it three-hundred-and-sixty degrees, and what comes out is a scoop of soft, off-white, spreadable cheese with a heavy layer of blue-grey fluff. It smells exactly the same as the prawn crackers he gets from the Wing Wah every Friday night.

In a weird way, the process is therapeutic, cleansing. He feels and looks cleaner, even though he doesn't smell it.

The relief at finally being able to scrape away the thick, matted caking between his buttocks was almost sexual, even though he does add to the vomit in the bath at seeing the crumbling Nutella on the butter knife.

Gently easing dried smegma from the bulb of his penis is an experience he never thought he would ever find arousing, and if not for the nauseating concoction brewing in the bath, he may have taken the opportunity to have a ninth jostle over the thought of Nicki and Ru Paul together.

He finishes with his feet; flakes of athlete's foot fall into the tub like snow, the garnish on the putrid jambalaya of his own, specially grown, ingredients. A breather is necessary before he begins the arduous task of shaving off all his body hair.

Vince sits on the toilet and thanks his genes that he isn't naturally hirsute. Balding from the exact moment he grew a full head of hair, anything south of his eyebrows has gathered like dust bunnies in hard-to-reach corners.

It is shocking how much fluff comes off him when he goes all over himself with the battery-operated razor. He can't help but smirk at how long it must have taken Henry to get rid of all his body hair; the man had been part-gorilla. He drops the hair into the bath, empties the razor head for good measure, uses an attachment just in case there are any nostril or ear hairs, wet-shaves everywhere with a pack of disposable razors, and sighs with relief that the second stage in the ritual's preparations is finally over.

Now comes the *really* gross part.

Chapter 13

Vince feels more naked than he has ever felt in his life. Despite not being a hairy man, he has never, ever before completely shaved - everywhere - down to the skin. It is akin to being reborn: his pores are open to the world; the heightened sensitivity is tantalising and scary at the same time. Especially considering what he is about to do.

The long-handled loofah only cost £1.49 from his local Wilko but it still pains him to lower it into the bath. Predominantly urine and faeces, the mixture is a rich, dark-orange, with clouds of brown where the excrement slowly dissolves.

As he stirs, harder bits of shit and flakes of yellow vomit cling to the loofah like lichen. Long butt-sausages sail across the surface while something dark and cephalopodic lurches through the piss at the bottom of the tub in time with his stirring.

When he is certain the stew is thoroughly mixed, he puts down the loofah, checks Henry's list of instructions, and prepares to climb in.

There are no verbal incantations in this ritual, it relies on endurance and the power of suggestion.

Vince clears his mind, aside from focusing on what he wants to rid from it. He visualises his own personification of Mr Hide, the beast within him that takes over when he gorges. He wonders what Mr Hide, that little voice, the tempter within, will look like when he's cast out.

A five-stone midget of me, his skin is rough with inflamed infection. He's my southern-fried baby. His skin is slick with boiling fat that seeps from every pore, pastry psoriasis between the wrinkles and rolls. His tongue's a wedge of fatty bacon slapping against candy-corn teeth, cackling, spitting melted cheese phlegm.

Vince begins the mantra inside his head thirty seconds before stepping over the rim of the bathtub.

Glut.

Glut.

Glut.

Glut.

Glut.

Vince dips a foot into the now luxuriously thick liquid and his bladder immediately releases over his thighs.

Glut.

Glut.

Glut.

Glut.

Glut.

At least it's warm.

Glut.

Glut.

Glut.

Glut.

Glut.

The turpid, slushy swill turns Vince to ice as he lowers himself, slowly, for fear of having a heart attack at the shock.

Glut.

Glut.

Glut.

Glut.

Glut.

Sludge clings like mud to his skin as he lies back and submerges, the urine level rising up to his armpits.

Glut.

Glut.

Glut.

Glut.

Glut.

Vince knows this won't be enough, knows the ritual calls for more.

He forces himself lower, deeper, into the bathtub, wedging himself tighter and tighter.

Glut.

Glut.

Glut.

Glut.

Gl–SHIT!

He is stuck.

He is fucking stuck.

Jammed in, both shoulders are fixed against the ceramic sides with just his face above piss level.

He screams and a log of epic proportions, speckled with dry-roasted peanuts, spaghetti and corn kernels slides into his mouth along with a throatful of the feculent fluid. Vince chomps the bloody thing in two, feeling it mash against his teeth, and tries to fight the panic, but something is happening inside his brain. Beyond his control, like a schizophrenic, he can hear it in his head still.

Glut.

Glut.

Glut.

Glut.

Glut.

He is short of breath.

Everything in his peripheral vision explodes into stars.

Vince is sure he is about to die.

The Glut

Chapter 14

As the stars disperse and begin to clear, there's nothing but weightlessness and pitch-black oblivion. If Vince is falling, he can't feel it.

So this is what it feels like to be dead.

With a complete absence of sensation, there is only awareness.

At least consciousness goes on.

Vince doesn't yet know if that's a blessing or a curse.

Gradually, like sunlight behind tightly closed eyelids, colour permeates the darkness, proving it is not as impenetrable as he thought.

A red star is the first thing he sees with these new eyes. It burns like an ember, just a pinprick in the velvet but giving off enough illumination to light this universe.

Vince feels then. He feels the cold of space, freezing temperature on his naked skin, his flesh goose-prickles, and frost blossoms. Something tugs at him, not at a hand or an arm or even at his body, but at his soul, and he starts to move through the void at an unnatural speed.

The red star gets bigger and brighter and the closer he gets the more sensation returns. The light hurts. It pulsates, bloody and tumorous.

It's Hell, oh my fucking god, I've died and I'm going to Hell.

If he has eyes, he can't close them, and the red radiation blinds until he is flung onto scorching black rock.

His skin bubbles and blisters as he touches the rough, volcanic surface and he hops a painful, never-ending rhumba to the backdrop of flames that leap as high as mountains. A rufescent sky ripples and bulges with dark clouds the colour of overripe plums, jagged red lightning slashing downward like a killer's stroke.

A rumble deep within the surface signals its arrival and Vince can hardly keep upright. He falls, burning his knees and elbows on steaming rock. Remnants of cooked morsels lie scattered around: charred bones and baked muscle.

It comes from nowhere, a planet-sized mound of sunburnt flesh. White fat spits from splits in its skin and an arm bigger than a city appears around its side. Frozen in disbelief and horror, Vince is plucked from the ground by skyscraper fingers and is back up in the sky.

Vince screams when he beholds The Glut in all its glory. It's bigger than he can comprehend.

Three arms push the colossal torso from a hole in the black rock and he is dangled over its gigantic face.

God-sized fingertips squeeze his torso.

Its black eyes are too small for it, but filled with greed and lust.

Its mouth goes on forever: there are worlds in there, and something that bears a close resemblance to our sun.

Everything is out of proportion.

Teeth and tusks and mandibles are just the beginning of what shreds the things it devours. There's stuff to pound and crush, a whole plethora of things to rend and tear.

A tongue as big and as wide as an ocean lolls idiotically, on it islands of infection, an archipelago of pus-filled blisters.

Its single horn, like an inverted question mark, moves with a life of its own as Vince is brought closer and closer to the epic point. He screams and screams and screams, the fumes from The Glut's breath blurring his vision in time for him to miss seeing the tip of the horn pierce him. But of course, he feels it. It enters him just below the scrotum and he is bisected, sliced open, but somehow still alert enough to feel everything fall out of his two halves before dropping into that all-consuming black hole.

Chapter 15

Vince hears screaming and it isn't until he feels pain in his throat that he realises he's the one doing it.

The stars clear and his vision comes back.

He forces his face upwards and spews up a torrent of faecal smoothie.

He's wedged tightly in the bath and shouts with everything he's got. He doesn't know whether what he's just seen was real or due to lack of oxygen, but right now, the important thing is to free himself.

He curses himself for the millionth time about getting himself into this situation, in lifestyle and size. Just because he is morbidly obese doesn't mean he has to spend his whole life cutting himself off from those he sees as normal people.

This near-death, it might even still *be death* experience has made him regret using his size as an excuse for everything. He has made an outcast of himself, not by what he put into his body but by what he hasn't let *out* of it.

It's true, like Henry said, *he's had one of those epiphanies.* Maybe the ritual has worked, or, more likely, he's realised how much of an epic fucking idiot he's been all his life, sticking this problem up on the biggest fucking pedestal in the world.

Vince moves his feet and the plug chain tickles his ankles. He tries to manoeuvre himself so he can hook a toe around it and pull it out; he fails at first, but on the fifth attempt, he yanks at it and out it comes.

It takes an age for the piss to drain from the bath, what with the other stuff clogging the plughole, but eventually the tide level drops enough for Vince to be able to rest his head back against the scum line.

Every thirty seconds, until his throat feels like it's bleeding, he screams for help with a fury he's never put into anything before.

He will get out.

Chapter 16

Vince wakes and he doesn't know if it's day or night. He's freezing. The ceramic is dry and he is coated with a thick grimy poultice, which is stiff against his skin. The smell in the bathroom has either lessened or he's become accustomed to it.

Hunger pangs rip up his guts.

His throat is harsh: sandpaper and broken glass. He tries to scream again but nothing will come out, he's all used up.

A belligerence possesses him like nothing he's ever encountered, a fight for survival, a stubborn tenacity. He will not go down. For the first time ever, he wants to live. Vince roars with the rage of it all, he would rather die trying than accept his fate. He pounds his feet against the bathtub and yells so loud that the stars come back — but he still doesn't quit.

Eventually, they come.

The caretaker, after the dozy fuckers next door finally complain about the racket, knocks on the front door repeatedly for a whole minute before he uses his brain and ears and opens the letterbox to listen.

Then the paramedics arrive and inevitably the fire brigade with some kind of saw to cut through the ceramic. Nothing is said about the unholy mess of sewerage Vince wallows in but their shocked expressions say enough. Vince doesn't care, though, he is happy, he is transformed, he has the power to change his life. He can see how stupidly desperate he must have been to fall for some ridiculous brainwashing jargon that a heavy metal nut probably got from the lyrics of a Cannibal Corpse song. The power to do this has been inside him all along.

Chapter 17

After an overnight stay in hospital, a week goes by and Vince doesn't try to eat healthier—he just does it without a second thought. The urges to gorge on high-fat or sugary foods have gone.

He busies himself by getting rid of everything unhealthy in his flat and distributing it to local food banks. He walks the trips too, ignoring the protests in his joints. He doesn't know how long he will have this new iron will and he plans to make the most of it.

On his way back from the food bank he sees a small blonde woman in a turquoise fleece handing out leaflets for the gym.

50% off your first month!

Without a moment's hesitation he accepts a flyer and pauses when the young girl smirks at him the same way as everyone else does.

"Sign me up now," he says, keeping his cool, smiling; it's not her fault, this kind of thing is ingrained in people.

"Excuse me?" she says, more than a little perplexed, possibly not altogether certain that this isn't the build-up to some lecherous joke.

"I want to join." Vince waves the flyer like a flag.

She smiles, sweet as honey, and all prejudice vanishes. She looks at him as though he's actually human and it feels amazing.

He notices she has the most exceptional silver eyes. They're supernatural.

"Oh, okay, I'm sorry, you took me by surprise. Most people don't even take the leaflets." Her laughter is lighter than snow.

"It's okay, I get that," Vince says, shocking himself: he's having a conversation with a real person. "Are you one of the trainers there?"

She shrugs, uncertain. "I am when people want someone other than the blokes that work there."

"Would you be able to train me?" Vince finds himself saying words that he never thought would come from his lips.

The woman chirps up a bit. "Mate, I can train anyone!"

Vince follows her a short way up the high street and they go inside the gym.

He signs up for a monthly membership and for the woman, Nicole, to train him three times a week.

He leaves feeling confident, on a massive high that seems to alleviate even the pain in his knees.

Vince still weighs thirty-two stones but his whole outlook on life has changed. He is determined to claw back what he can. Something inside him has switched from off to on after the ridiculous ordeal he has put himself through.

He starts to take pride in things. Buys himself a fitness tracking smart watch, downloads fitness apps with nutritional advice and information, and catalogues everything he is doing.

Everything in the first week is unbelievably perfect.

Then he finds the lump.

Chapter 18

He notices it in the shower at the gym.

It's the size, shape and colour of a kidney bean; when he touches it, he can feel it pulsating as though it has a tiny heartbeat inside.

Nicole has put him through his paces and he's freshening up when he touches it and sees its reflection in the shower's tempered-glass door.

It's not sore or itchy so he's not too bothered, just curious. Without a proper mirror, he can't inspect it anyway. Weight clinic is the following day so he makes a mental note to show the doctor there, even though they will probably, like he seems to do with 99% of ailments, put it down to Vince's size.

He remembers a time when he overheard — the whole waiting room overheard — an altercation between Doctor Russell and Henry Green, and Henry, the *old* Henry had yelled, "I could get my fucking dick cut off with a pair of shears and you'd say it was because I was too fat!" It wasn't far from the truth.

The bane of his childhood, well, his life so far, regarding health professionals, was that no matter the problem, no matter the symptoms, they would mention his weight. As though he wasn't constantly aware of it.

Vince wanted to stick it to them, he wanted to be a success like the crazy Henry Green.

If he could, and if he was successful, he wanted to help others like him too.

Doctor Russell is the human embodiment of Slenderman, nine feet tall with an arm span that enables him to slap both sides of a twelve-foot room at once. His scalp reflects the overhead strip lights, and he is the skinniest, most willowy person Vince knows.

That's what makes this part of weight clinic hard, the fact that Doctor Russell is only able to show empathy towards his clients which is usually laced with an underlying condescension.

He dons blue latex gloves and gets Vince to lift his clothing when he mentions his unusual blemish.

After prodding and poking for all of ten seconds he deems it to be a pressure sore, prescribes a barrier cream and some antibiotics, and tells him to pop on the scales. He says it so casually, as if it means nothing.

Vince dreads the phrase, it doesn't matter how they say it, how they flower it up, it always makes him tremble inside.

So, how much will it be this time?

Vince kicks off his shoes, steps onto the platform, stares ahead, and waits for the outcome.

Doctor Russell bends down to read the screen and lets out a loud, solitary laugh of disbelief. "You've lost a stone."

"You're joking?"

"No," Doctor Russell says, excitement over. "Whatever it is you've been doing, carry on."

"I joined a gym," Vince says proudly, "started eating healthier."

"Good man, good man. Keep it up."

"I'm going to." Vince puts his shoes back on and heads towards the door.

"Maybe you'll be the next Henry Green."

He turns around and sees the doctor smiling at him.

Did Henry tell him about his mad beliefs?

Vince sits back down. "Did Henry ever actually say how he lost his weight? I mean, he was always quite secretive with me and the others."

Something crosses Doctor Russell's face and his happy demeanour falters for a second.

"Oh, I can't recall exactly what," he says, flapping a long-fingered hand Vince's way, "I think it was some self-meditative tomfoolery. But it's whatever works for the individual, Vince."

"Thanks, Doctor." Vince leaves with a spring in his step, it's the incentive he needs to help him to carry on.

He makes sure not to hide his exuberance in front of the others in the waiting room. "I lost a stone," he says, to no one in particular.

They all smile, most of them genuinely so.

He hopes it will show them that there is hope: if he can do it, anyone can.

Chapter 19

When Vince gets home, he strips off down to his pants and stands in front of a mirror before taking a full body photograph, face-on and then sideways.

Even though he cannot see where this stone has gone, he's immensely proud and ecstatic.

It's when he's using an app to edit his *before* photo that he notices the strange mark on his belly again.

It looks bigger.

He moves closer to the mirror and is almost certain it has grown.

There's still no discomfort, though, and he trusts the doctor's diagnosis.

He changes into his gym wear, grabs his crutches, and goes to his lesson with Nicole.

His path takes him past The Triffid. The pub is busy with patrons going in and out so he automatically crosses the road to avoid any jibes they might feel like offering.

Someone calls his name and breaks off from a small group of people.

It's Henry.

He looks like he's bulked up on muscle even more and Vince still can't believe it's the same man that used to be heavier than him.

"Vince," Henry says, happy to see him, even though the last time they met, they parted with a fist fight.

"Hello, Henry," Vince answers uneasily, not certain how to greet this man — who might be a complete lunatic.

"You're looking good, new threads, man?"

Henry points at Vince's tracksuit.

"Oh, yeah, I joined the gym."

Henry laughs, "Ha, good one!"

"No, I really did."

Henry's eyes widen in surprise. "Oh, wow. That's good. It'll help with what comes next."

"What comes next? What do you mean?"

"Yeah," Henry says, checking for unwanted listeners, "now that you've performed the ritual."

Vince laughs in Henry's face. It just comes out; he doesn't mean to be rude. "I didn't do the ritual."

Now it's Henry's turn to laugh. "I saw you a couple of weeks back."

"Where?" Vince asked, shocked, knowing full well he stayed at home during his ritual preparations.

"You answered the door to Uber Eats."

"You were watching me?"

Henry ignores his question. "You were filthy."

There's no point in denying it, so he doesn't bother. "Okay," Vince begins, "so I fell for your devil worshipping shite. So what? I was in a bad place. The lowest I had ever been. But it showed me just how desperate I was, how fucking stupid I was to even consider such crap."

Henry shrugs. "But you still did it? Waited out the six weeks? Followed all the procedures for the ritual preparations?"

"Yes! Yes, I did. There, you happy now? You've had your laugh, go and tell all your new friends how you got me to make an absolute fucking tramp of myself. But it wasn't for nothing, oh no, because when I performed your pathetic ritual, I got stuck in the fucking bath, passed out, and almost died. And when I came to, I realised how much of a prick I had been all my life." Vince looks at his feet so Henry can't see the emotion on his face. "But do you know what? It's worked, because I've started eating healthier, joined a gym, and lost a stone. It's me doing this, not some daft ritual."

"Yeah," Henry says sympathetically, "that's what I thought at first, too."

Vince turns in disgust and begins to walk away.

No way is Henry going to ruin this for me, no way.

"Vince, please, wait," Henry calls out as Vince storms off. He gives chase.

"I'm not listening to anymore of your crap, Henry." Vince stops and leans on a crutch. "I'm happy this alternative therapy, or whatever the hell you think it was, works for you, I really am, but I do not believe in that shit. I'm sorry, Henry."

"It doesn't really matter whether you believe it or not, mate. You've already done it."

Vince shakes his head. "No, no, no! I acted like a complete bell-end and showed myself how desperate I was to beat this thing inside of me and the levels I was prepared to stoop to in order to achieve that. And that if I could have the determination to make such a bloody mess of myself, I've got it in me to achieve anything. Anything."

"Mate," Henry is close to tears, "I really wish that was the case, but it's not. It's not you. All you have done is performed an ancient separation ritual, isolating the part of your psyche that makes you compulsively eat and allowing it to take on human form."

"What? What?" Vince needs Henry to repeat what he's just said in case he's misheard his acquaintance's new descent into another dimension of madness.

Henry grits his teeth and looks ashamedly away. "All you have done is performed an ancient ritual, isolating the part of your psyche that makes you compulsively eat and allowing it to take on human form."

Vince is unable to control it. His laughter hits Henry in the face like a nuclear blast and Vince feels like the world's cruellest bully, but he can't help it. His crutches creak as he leans over them, convulsing with raucous shrieks at Henry's Jekyll and Hyde bullshit.

Henry's the colour of a Red Delicious apple; if this were a cartoon, smoke would shoot out of each ear in scalding jets. "To hell with you."

Vince tries to shout an apology to the rapidly retreating Henry, but he's still catching his breath and trying his hardest not to continue thinking about what Henry has just told him. It's the funniest, stupidest thing he's ever heard, like something out of a really trashy, only-written-for-the-cash bizarro novel.

The Glut

Chapter 20

"Right." Vince is still chuckling after his encounter with Henry on the street when he greets Nicole in the gym. "What are we doing today?"

Nicole, as ever, is a vibrant, Duracell bunny of energy. It's ridiculous at any time of day but it's infectious and endearing. "Okay, Vinny, today, I thought I'd get you on the treadmill seeing as you've been telling me that you've been walking more."

Vince goes cold at the prospect of getting on such an advanced piece of machinery. He's seen people on them, glazed in sweat, running as though they have the devil on their back. He can't do that. He tells her as much.

"You told me you've had X-rays done recently, yeah?"

Vince nods.

"And the quack says the only issues he can find with your knees is your weight?"

"Pretty much."

Nicole nods. "Okay, then. Hear me out. I'm a firm believer that everyone can run. No matter how big, little, young or old you are, anyone can. And you can learn at any age."

Vince mutters a sceptical, "Okay."

"What I want you to do is to step onto the treadmill, without your crutches, and find a pace that's comfortable for you to walk at. Do you think you can do that?"

Vince nods and gingerly puts the toe of a trainer on the standing plates either side of the running belt, as though it will collapse beneath his weight.

"It's not going to break."

"Don't be so sure," Vince says, stepping onto the machine.

"This model holds a maximum of 500 pounds."

"That's not much heavier than me," Vince says with some embarrassment.

Nicole jumps up on the treadmill beside him and fixes him with her intensely grey eyes. "Everyone has to start somewhere, and we are going to do this!"

They really are horror movie eyes, Vince thinks, and starts up the manual programme.

Once he's used to how the thing works, he finds a speed that matches his walking pace, doesn't try to impress the gorgeous woman at his side like any other bloke would, and walks.

It's a weird sensation, walking without getting anywhere, but he immediately likes the way, once in the rhythm of things, he can switch off what his body is doing and almost move on autopilot.

A few minutes pass. Nicole jogs off to the other side of the gym to do whatever, and then returns.

"Right, Vinny, let's up the speed a little. My rule for beginners is two-and-a-half over what they're walking at. So, let's see." She leans over to peer at his screen and alters the speed on his treadmill.

He feels the running belt begin to go quicker. At first, he tries to walk quicker, then he naturally falls into a slow jog.

"That's it!" Nicole shouts and claps, "you're doing it. Now try and do that for as long as you can and when you want to stop, nod and I'll hit the stop button."

Her enthusiasm is contagious and he gives it his all. He's out of breath almost instantly; he feels like he's going to have a heart attack but he carries on regardless. *Just move your arms and legs*, he tells himself, *and ignore the wobble*.

When he can fight no more, when his knees feel like balls of molten lead and he feels like he will actually die, he nods and Nicole keeps her promise and hits the stop button.

Vince grabs hold of the treadmill's sides for dear life, praying that he won't throw up all over the expensive equipment.

"You have got this, baby!" Nicole bounces up and down, hollering, holding out her palm for a high-five.

Vince is frozen somewhere between a punch and a marriage proposal.

The man who staggers, dripping wet, into the changing rooms is a different person than the one who entered the gym an hour before. Every part of him aches, there are aches in muscles he has never even felt before.

It feels amazing, he feels as though he could punch straight through a brick wall like the *Incredible Hulk*. Like a barbarian who has just come off a body-strewn battlefield covered in the blood, sweat, and internal juices of his enemies.

He stands in front of the mirror and doesn't see a deformed, gross pile of wobbling red fat like he would have done a month ago, he sees a work in progress, the start of something magnificent.

Vince roars and pounds his chest—a veritable King Kong.

I

Fucking

Jogged.

"Stupid prick," an old man mutters as he walks past. Vince has seen him on the rowing machine, gently rowing as if he's on a fucking lake wooing Nora Batty and trying to get inside her wrinkled tights. Vince is a warrior, he goes at it like he wants to die doing it, it's the only way to be successful, he knows that now. Do it, or die trying.

Vince smiles at his reflection, knows that it will be changing rapidly. In Nicole's words, he has got this, baby.

He has got this baby, or at least that's what it looks like, the same as when you see photos of prenatal babies in the womb. His red mark has grown, it's still bean-shaped but it's doubled in size. And it looks like a foetus. Vince touches it with his fingertip, it's about the size of a cherry tomato, raised out from the skin, claret in colour and completely smooth. He can feel his pulse beat in it and is instantly nauseated.

Oh, fucking hell, it's cancer, I know it. It's all he can think of.

His scalp prickles with fear and he irrationally blames his newly-caught cancer on being foul for one-and-a-half months and subsequently bathing in it.

Rationality begins to surface and he tells himself that it has to be a rash of some kind for it to have grown so bloody quickly in such a short space of time.

It must have been this size earlier on when Doctor Russell examined it.

A pressure sore, that's all.

He applies a liberal amount of the barrier cream, pops an antibiotic, and even slaps a dressing over it for good measure.

Once again, he's proud of himself for his quick thinking, his refusal to dwell on things and let the darker side of his moods take over. He holds his head up high, gets dressed, looks at his reflection triumphantly, and walks back on to the gym floor.

The news is on the screens, they're on about the comet again. He'd almost forgotten about that.

It's got a name now: Frenzel, after the student Adele Frenzel, who discovered it.

Vince thinks it's quite cool to have a comet named after you, and he's glad it's a uni student rather than some old fart like Patrick Moore, well, supposing it's a *young* university student.

They are spouting jargon about when she first spotted it, when it will be visible in the skies, and where to look.

He feels a presence beside him and someone nudges his shoulder.

"You gonna wish on it, mate?" It's Nicole.

"I know absolutely fuck-all about astronomy. Can you wish on comets?" he says, keeping his eyes on the screen.

"I bloody well wish on fireworks, mate," Nicole says with a giggle, and nudges him in the ribs. "You did great today."

Vince leaves feeling even lighter.

Chapter 22

He's already noticing the differences since losing the weight.

His clothes are looser and he's waking up less in the night because of his sleep apnoea. He is better-rested because of the gym and all the aching muscles.

Deep Heat has become his friend; after a moderate abs workout, his stomach protests when he lies down and the muscles stretch. He simultaneously cries out and laughs.

In spite of the pain, there is a feeling of achievement.

No pain, no gain.

He finally understands the age-old cliché.

"Fuck!" Vince screams himself awake from a dream of something evil and red.

His stomach is on fire. There's a glowing poker sliding through his abdominal wall and it's slowly being rotated. That's what it feels like.

He reels with the agony.

I've torn a muscle, that's all.

He can't take his hands off it. He scrunches himself up in a ball. Something squirms in his belly like a snake unfurling, and the pain spreads from his lower abdomen to his chest.

A heart attack. That's just fucking typical now I've finally knocked this shit on the head.

He manages to pry a hand from his gut to snatch at his mobile phone; his fingertips just touch it when a tearing sensation makes him slap the thing across the room. He yowls in excruciating torture: through streaming eyes he half-expects to see a xenomorph poking its little bald head out of his belly.

He is paralysed as he watches his stomach begin to move involuntarily.

Something curved presses against the flesh behind the pressure sore and the purple blemish starts to bleed dark red blood.

It splits.

A mauve lump pushes its way through the open sore, his skin and muscle parting as it forces its way upwards and out of him.

Spherical, he knows immediately what it is, but his mind finds it difficult to comprehend,

The baby's eyes are open, which somehow makes the nightmarish scenario even worse, and they're completely black.

Its tiny mouth puckers with the exertion of having to perform its own birth.

A little hand appears with tiny black fingernails like a baby goth, then another. They push and pull and prise apart the fissure and it lets out a triumphant little squeal as it squeezes out its shoulders.

Vince feels its feet pedalling and kicking for purchase inside him, pummelling his bladder and bowel, which release themselves violently on the bedsheets.

An umbilical cord protrudes from the baby's navel, the other end lost somewhere inside the visceral explosion whence it burst.

Vince shrieks and ejects a hot, yellow torrent of gutwash spray in his newborn baby's face. A baptism in vomit. He tugs at the hideous umbilical cord, endures the unholy sensation of it pulling his internal organs, and the pain makes him grey around the edges. He flops back on the blood-slicked bed and screams blue murder. He wants to pass out, die, the pain is so intense.

The baby gets its feet out and its little hands grip the rubbery snake joining them.

With unnatural strength, it pulls and Vince realises it's growing out of his intestines: it's a coil of his guts, not an umbilical cord.

He sees the slippery, squamous rope stretch between the baby's hands as it tries to pull it all out of him. A magician's knotted handkerchief trick springs to mind and Vince feels his sanity unravelling along with his guts.

The baby's minute penis dribbles into the desolation of its birth hole.

Aw, it's a boy! The madness in Vince chitters and when his son lifts the coil of intestine up to his mouth and begins gumming at it with ravenous enthusiasm, Vince finally, mercifully, passes out.

Chapter 23

He's naked when he wakes and he can tell by the light streaming in between the curtains that it's later than usual. His palms slap to his stomach. There is no pain and the mysterious kidney bean blemish has faded considerably. Vince is about to tell himself it was all a horrible dream when his hand flops down onto the tacky sheets and comes up covered in congealing blood.

He sits up.

He is spotless, it's as though someone picked him up and plonked him down on a butcher's slab whilst he was asleep.

His natural, rational mind tries to make sense of the copious amounts of dried blood.

Did the pressure sore burst?

Could all that have come from such a small wound?

He examines the pink patch to see if there's any signs of a scab or an opening. There isn't. A clutter comes from the kitchen and he remembers his dream in more detail.

No.

Vince walks across his bedroom, still starkers, metal crutch over his shoulder like a baseball bat.

Rustling comes from the kitchen cupboards.

He turns into the hallway and sees thick slug-trails of blood and black stuff on the lino. It stinks.

There's a tiny red handprint on the white gloss of the kitchen door. He hears plastic bags being torn apart, food exploding over the floor.

I've got fucking Gremlins.

All he needs now is for Bing fucking Crosby to start singing *Do You Hear What I Hear?* and the last little seed pod of his sanity will blow away into the ether, never to be seen again.

Greedy slopping noises come instead, and that seed just wafts away.

Vince, all thirty-one stones of naked insanity, launches himself at the kitchen door, crutch raised high.

His battle cry peters out into a pathetic mewling as he throws open the door and sees the baby on the kitchen floor.

It's twice as big as its birth-size already and covered in a variety of different condiments.

Smashed jars and emptied containers circle it; it seems oblivious to the chunks of broken glass that are brought up to its mouth amidst the gloopy handfuls of mayonnaise, ketchup, and mustard.

The stuff drools from its mouth and Vince doesn't know if it's swallowing the glass and is impervious to pain or whether its anatomy is abnormal.

It's grossly overweight for a newborn, but this makes it bigger, tougher, more dexterous. Its mouth opens and Vince is sure he sees the nubs of teeth.

It repulses him.

A puddle of stinking beige surrounds it as it continuously shits whilst loading the opposite end with mechanical synchronicity.

Vince looks at the heavy metal arm clasp of the crutch and raises it. The baby holds a tiny palm upward as if to ward off the killing blow, and its filthy mouth moves. "Daddy!"

"How the fuck can you speak already?"

It doesn't say anything else, lowering its hand as he drops the crutch. He can't kill it: it's a baby, no matter where it came from, the nature of its conception and however the fuck it was born, it is a baby.

Well, he thinks, *more of a toddler now.*

It paws at the mulch of assorted colours on the floor, lifts more to its mouth.

"Food," it says, as it glops through the slime.

"Oh my God," Vince mutters, finding it hard to believe what he's about to do. "Come on, let's get you cleaned up and I'll make you something proper to eat."

The baby takes him in and its expression is old beyond its years. Its eyes are more human-like now, the sclera now white but the pupils and iris impenetrable black pools.

It raises a chunky pair of arms that resemble bread rolls. "Daddy!"

Chapter 24

Vince carries the baby through the hallway at arm's length. Aside from the rapid growth and the ability to develop speech within hours of its birth, it looks just like a normal baby boy.

It's hard for him not to think of it as an *it*, though, as there's nothing natural about this baby.

A small part of him, even though he knows it's ludicrous, wonders whether he was somehow drugged and someone planted their kid on him.

The baby's hands open and close, reaching his fat little arms towards Vince, beckoning him to cradle him properly. But he can't. The kid is covered in gunk and he still doesn't quite know what he's going to do with him.

The baby's mouth opens and lets out an ear-piercing shriek. His tiny teeth have broken all the way through the gums now.

"Shhh," Vince begins and the baby's legs wrap around his wrists with unnatural dexterity, as though they're made of rubber. Vince recoils and lets go.

The baby somersaults between Vince's arms, hanging upside down for a second before twisting his torso around 360 degrees and grabbing handfuls of the fat that hangs below Vince's left tricep. Vince gasps in pain as the entire weight of the baby hangs from his underarm.

The baby springs onto Vince's chest, he falls back into a wall, and together they slide to the floor. He tries to push the rabid baby off as it snaps its jaws at him.

It's a fucking zombie. It's all he can think of.

He can't shake it off, it's slippery with the mess it made—and too strong. His fingers slip, he loses purchase, and the little 'un's mouth clamps down on his belly like a plunger.

Casting aside all thoughts of not being able to hurt him because he's a baby, Vince beats his fists at the thing's head.

It's not a he, it's most definitely an it. A fucking monster.

It looks—and feels—as though it's trying to give him a love bite, its tiny hands grabbing great doughy chunks of Vince's tummy fat, its little blackened fingernails digging into his flesh.

Vince yelps, and then feels a sharp scratch where the kid's mouth sucks, and a numbness begins to spread over his stomach as if it's injected him with an anaesthetising venom. He continues to push at the baby but it's latched on, barnacle-tight, blood and yellow fat seeping out from the sides of its mouth. The sound it makes is akin to a vacuum cleaner sucking up vomit and Vince can see it visibly grow as it eats.

For what seems like hours, it stays there welded to his side, and then without any warning it rolls onto the floor, belly extended, a clown-smile of yellow clumps and grease around its bloodied lips. Its eyes are heavy and lethargic, and within seconds it's asleep.

Vince crawls away from it completely traumatised.

He shuts himself in his bedroom and weighs up his options. He sees in the mirror that there's a small mark like a love bite where the baby attached itself— but that's not all, the flab from that side of his stomach has flattened, the skin now saggier, hanging.

"What the fuck?" Vince quickly finds and throws on clothes; he needs to escape whilst the bloody thing is asleep.

This is all Henry's fault, with his fucking rituals.

He never said anything about summoning a god-awful, fat-sucking, lipo-sucking demon.

Chapter 25

It's when he's racing down the street, one hand clutched on the deflated area of his stomach that he realises he has left the crutches at home and there is currently no pain in his knees. He allows himself a brief moment to congratulate himself, a mental pat on the back for the weight he's lost and his hard work at the gym, and then he hears Henry's voice saying, *Yeah, that's what I thought, too.*

None of his success has been his own doing and he is crestfallen.

All you have done is performed an ancient isolation ritual, isolating the part of your psyche that makes you compulsively eat and allow it to take on human form.

"Fucking Jekyll and Hyde bullshit," Vince spits angrily and punches the nearest window which happens to belong to his friends at the Vaggie Dulux takeaway. They run out in unison; the one in charge who always does the talking recognises him immediately.

"My friend, what is the matter?" He looks solemnly out of dark eyes beneath black eyebrows so thick they join in the middle. Vince thinks he sounds like a cartoon vampire.

"Nothing," Vince mumbles, and tries to push past.

"It's not nothing, you hit the glass. What is wrong? Come in. We are friends, no?" The cartoon vampire puts his hand on Vince's shoulder. "We have a special offer on stuffed crust today."

Vince swipes the man's hand off his shoulder. "No. Leave me alone. You can stuff your stuffed crust."

The cartoon vampire sighs as though it's the saddest thing in the world. "Any time you want to come back, my friend."

Vince walks off, leaving them to converse in another language.

In the northern sky, like the news said, he can make out the tiny comet as it whizzes around the planet. It's barely visible to the naked eye, but they say it'll get a lot closer over the next few weeks. He wishes he wasn't so scared and angry, then he could stand and look at it longer.

There's no pull as he walks past takeaway after takeaway but he can't even claim that resistance as his own.

A heavy depression seeps in as he arrives at Henry's door. He thumps on it as though hates the fucking thing and hears panicked swearing coming from within.

Good.

Chapter 26

Henry's having a heated debate with someone inside and it warms Vince's heart to think of the man who landed him in this shit being in distress. The shouting escalates into decipherable volumes and he hears the words "Get back in there, you fat bastard!" followed by the sound of something breaking.

Not worried in the slightest that he is interrupting a domestic between Henry and a possible lover, Vince hammers on the door again, then for some reason he remembers his first fleeting visit and how a voice from behind a closed door had called 'Daddy.'

Oh my God.

Vince starts kicking at the door until he hears Henry begin to unfasten the locks.

"Oh, it's you." Keeping the chain on, Henry peeps through the gap. Vince can see a trickle of blood on his forehead and he smiles.

"Hey, Henry."

"What is it?" Henry says. In the background comes the crash-bang of furniture being thrown around, plates smashing.

Vince delights in his discomfort. "Are you busy right now?"

There's a hollow thunk as some projectile whacks off the back of Henry's head; his eyes cross a little.

"Bear, yest a lit," he says all wrong.

"Can I come in?" Vince asks and motions to the chain.

Henry snaps out of his daze and panic sets in. "No! Now's not a good ti–"

One moment he's there, and another, he's gone.

Vince stares wide-eyed at the few inches of Henry's flat he can see. He hears the sounds of fighting and even though he doesn't give two shits about the guy, he can't stand by and let Henry be beaten up. He takes a few steps back and runs, slamming his shoulder into the door, busting the chain from its fittings and sending it clattering away.

Henry is wrestling with an extremely hairy, extremely naked man. The naked man is on top and is trying his best to pin both of Henry's hands down in one of his own. He's bigger than Henry, about three or four stones overweight, long black hair hanging down so Vince is unable to see his face.

"Oi," Vince shouts, hoping that will be enough to deter the turd, but Henry's assailant continues. Henry's knee repeatedly goes up between the man's legs, crushing his dangling testicles, but he doesn't even notice.

Vince quickly looks around the hallway; the only thing that could be used as a makeshift weapon is a freestanding hat-and-coat stand which seems to be being used as a bag tree. He grabs it and thrusts the wide base forwards like a knight's lance.

Vince runs down the hallway and when the base of the hatstand connects with the attacker's hairy chest, he finally acknowledges Vince's existence — and Vince sees that the attacker is also Henry. *What the fucking shit? There's two of them? Is this invasion of the pod people or some shit?*

Henry jumps up off the floor and together they pin the other Henry against the wall.

Other Henry is just like old-Henry before the weight loss, fat and Rasputin-like but nowhere near as overweight as Henry had been.

This is his Mr Hide, his glut-demon.

Other Henry thrashes like a man possessed, a vampire being staked at sunrise; yellowed teeth thick with plaque gnash at the air as he reaches out and tries to claw.

Vince feels the wood start to give.

"We need to get him in his room," Henry says, and points to a dark, open doorway.

They give Other Henry a little slack, just enough for him to come unstuck from the wall, then shove him towards the room. The strength of the Other Henry is unbelievable and when they get him through the doorway, he grabs the hatstand right out of their hands. Luckily for them, he falls backwards over something that, even in the half-light, looks like a body.

Henry slams the door shut and fastens the bolts on the reinforced door before collapsing in exhaustion.

Angry banging comes from the door behind him, followed by a pathetic farmyard bleating. "Daddy, pleeeease, I'm 'ungry!"

"Dude," Vince slumps to the floor too, "I believe in you, bro." The laughter that comes from him is almost as scary as the situation they're in.

Chapter 27

They both sit there listening to naked flesh slap against metal as Other Henry repeatedly throws himself at the door, falls, takes a run-up and does it all over again.

Vince decides to break the ice. "So…"

Henry sits with his back against the shuddering door, face buried in his hands.

"What's going on?" Vince asks.

Henry scowls at him through blood streams that come from a head wound that seems to be clotting. "What the fuck do you think? It is what I said it was."

"But that in there is a crazed lunatic."

Henry nods. "Yeah, I know. He's just hungry. He never, ever stops eating. He's always so fucking hungry."

Vince thinks about what, in theory, Henry claims to have done, separated the part of himself that excessively eats and given it its own individual body. He has effectively given life to something that is only interested in consumption. At least when it was a part of Henry, no matter how tiny, there was another part that stopped to eating.

"How the hell have you coped so far?" Vince asks, remembering the abundance of food that lined the hallway on his first visit, and acknowledging that now there's nothing left. "Let me guess, you can't afford it?"

Henry's eyes flare for a second. "Do you have any money you can lend me? I'm due some soon."

"Why should I lend you any money? You've landed me in the same situation as you!"

Henry waves his hands over his new physique. "There are still benefits. Pros that outweigh the cons, Vince, and you owe me."

"Owe you? What the fuck do I owe you?"

"I've helped you! You have nothing stopping you from becoming like me, now." Henry pauses and points as if he can see through the bricks and mortar. "You've joined the gym, you have the strongest willpower ever now, thanks to me, and I didn't even fucking charge you like I did the-" Henry cuts himself off and says *fuck* five times.

"What? *The others?* The others, Henry?" Vince shouldn't be surprised, if this thing works as well as Henry claims it does, and he's living proof, then people would pay through the nose. "Oh my God, Henry. You're making a business out of this? Shit. Shit. How many? How many poor fat bastards are going to give fucking birth to their little gluttonous baby doppelgangers in the middle of the night? What happens when they can't afford to feed them? What happens then, Henry? Huh?"

Henry mutters something into his chest.

"What?"

He lifts his face and fear blanches it." The Other consumes them and they go back to how they were."

Vince's alien hysterics are back now at full volume.

"I tried killing it," Henry confesses, "when it was just a toddler. I slit its throat whilst it ate ice cream." He laughs, "Really deep, too, as you could see it running out every time he swallowed."

"Oh my God!"

"They aren't made the same as us–"

"No fucking shit."

"I think they're little bits of the thing that we perform the ritual to. The Glut. I think what we're actually doing is freeing the seeds it plants in every living person and basically giving them a life of their own."

"And still you say it's a good thing?"

"It is. *For us*. All we have to do is find a way to control them," Henry smiles hopefully, "and keep them satisfied. When they get fatter, we get thinner. It's why the gym is important. I don't think they can take away our muscles."

"How many, Henry? How many people have you done this to?" Vince shouts so loud the racket from the bedroom temporarily stops.

"Five," he says, in hardly a whisper.

"Jesus Christ, the poor bastards. People from our clinic?"

Henry shakes his head urgently, "No, no, you were the only one from there, aside from me."

"I feel so special. So, what did you do, go around the local areas hanging around outside weight loss classes, or what?"

"There was only one other person like us, who had eating problems." Henry's face fell.

"*Was*, Henry? I couldn't help but notice you used past tense there. Where is this person now?"

Henry shrugs. "She couldn't keep up with her avatar's demands."

"Avatar? You make them sound so fucking cute, like a bloody emoji."

"It kept feeding off her..."

Vince reflexively touches the patch on his belly where the baby had sucked the fat out of him.

"...there was barely anything left last time I went around to check on her. And then..."

"And then?"

"And then a few weeks went past and I saw her exactly the way she had been before she took part in the ritual preparations. Obese." Henry stares off into space. "They become one again, and it's all been for nothing, but do we really know who's in charge anymore, inside?"

"Fucking hell." Vince can say no more. This has gone from Jekyll and Hyde to Invasion of the Fucking Body Snatchers.

Henry perks up. "But it's okay, Vince, it's okay. It's going to be okay, I promise. It was all trial and error, then. Me and the other three have been working together, we've been planning what to do."

"How? How the hell can you control such insatiable monsters?" Vince is aching from sitting on the floor so he gets up.

"We keep them prisoner." Henry's face is alive with excitement. "There's at least one of the avatars that can use the other three. Plus, they literally can't be destroyed."

Vince doesn't like what he's hearing. "You said there was only one other person with eating problems and they're now out of the picture, yeah?"

"Yeah."

"So, what about the others? Who are they? What are their names?"

Henry shakes his head, "No, I've told you too much already. You will never have to worry about money again. If you're in on this, you're in all the way, if not, you can take your Mini-You and scarper. I've told you what you need to do."

"I'll tell the fucking cops, man, go to the newspapers. You won't get away with this shit."

"Even if you did, you won't find us. Do you honestly think anyone would believe this bollocks? You don't even know who the others are."

Vince thinks about Henry's transformation and about the twenty stones of excess weight that still clings to his own body and how it's slowly drowning him in a cesspit of his own making.

So fucking what if it's cheating? Maybe it's the only way I'll get out of this fucking fat suit alive! The damage is done, there is no going back.

"Okay, I'm in."

Chapter 28

When they get fatter, we get thinner. It's why the gym is important. I don't think they can take away our muscles.

Avatars.

Even though he hates what Henry calls them, the name sticks in his head. Vince's avatar is costing stupid amounts of money but luckily the worst kinds of foods are the cheapest. After the battle at Henry's, Vince paid a visit to the nearest DIY shop for a heavy chain and a padlock. His avatar has been chained ever since. He has to fight the urges inside him, telling him what he was doing was wrong, that he was locking up a child.

He isn't a child. *It* isn't a child.

Three weeks later, he — it — is the size of a teenager.

It's weird looking at it.

It huddles by the radiator, occasionally testing the chain links to try to free himself.

Vince is grateful that, considering how impervious to pain they seem to be, it hasn't attempted to gnaw off its own foot to escape.

It resembles a younger Vince, but a Vince that never was, a skinnier one.

At that age, Vince weighed more in stones than his age in years. The turning point for that secret game he played with himself was when he rocketed to ten stone at the age of nine. His avatar is the teenage Vince who ate a little bit too much, probably played video games instead of going out with his friends, but who wasn't grossly overweight. Whereas he had been the opposite back then: he was never indoors, was forever outside playing, walking, biking, hanging with the one or two equally outcast friends – and yet *he* was the one who only got bigger and bigger, like James's peach.

The avatar is the twin that time forgot and Vince hates it. It represents everything that's ruined his life so far. For no reason other than his own sick satisfaction, Vince steps across the room and kicks it in the face as it bites thick white chunks from a block of lard.

The avatar's teeth click shut and a half-inch sliver of tongue plops onto the floor along with the fat. He scoops up the tip of flesh and bloody grease, smooshes it back into his ever-working mouth and chew, chew, chews.

Its eyes are dull, matted things, heavy-lidded as though it's drugged. Milky drool runs freely from the corners of its mouth. It looks bored as fuck.

Vince can't help but think that this is exactly what he used to look like, back in his bingeing days.

"You fucking wasted the first thirty-five years of my life, you cunt!" Vince screams at the automatic fat-disposal unit. It helps having something to direct his rage and resentment towards. He kicks it again, in the shoulder, careful not to get any of the bodily filth on his new trainers.

He falls on his back, still chew, chew, chewing, then reaches and unwraps another block of lard. Lard is all he buys it now: cheap, economy, awful-smelling lard. Blocks of it line the walls. It doesn't have a chance to melt.

The room is vile. Yellow streaks of shit paint the walls and have soaked into the carpet and there is a mountain of trash. It doesn't matter, Vince knows they're moving the avatars soon.

He'll clean up then.

"See you later, Glut-Bucket," Vince says, kicking the thing in the kneecap and delighting in the sound of crunching bones. "Going to the gym."

Vince is in love with the gym. He's become a new kind of junkie; loves the endorphins it gives him. Nicole is over the moon with how he's progressing and he insists it's all down to her, which she finds flattering but insists it's not.

They've struck up a good friendship, great banter, and she even retaliates to one or two flirtatious jokes he has made. Another couple of stones and Vince reckons he'll be in there.

He can run three kilometres without stopping to walk, and every time he goes that little bit further, doesn't matter how sweaty he is, Nicole gets so excited she hugs him. He loves feeling her boobs press against him and he can't wait to wank in the shower afterwards.

Yeah, he loves the gym.

Chapter 29

It's been two months since Vince has seen Henry and although he's been expecting his call, he's still surprised to find him waiting behind the Tesco delivery man when he opens his front door.

Vince takes the four boxes of lard from the driver, ignores his befuddled expression and ushers Henry in. He's looking well, a lot less stressed. They wait for the Tesco guy to do his thing and leave before going inside.

"Today's the day, Vince," Henry says with feverish gusto. "Where is it? Your avatar?"

Henry's wearing an all-black, three-piece suit that looks expensive as fuck. Something has changed in the last few weeks, for the better.

Vince points to a heavily-bolted door.

"How big is he? Roughly?" Henry asks casually.

Vince shrugs and holds out his palm, level with his eyes.

"No, in weight and approximate age if he were human."

Vince considers the weight he's lost and tries his best to estimate his avatar's mass. "Probably about sixteen stone, looks like he's in his mid-twenties."

Henry nods enthusiastically and presses his phone. "Hey, yeah, Donna. Yeah, it's Henry."

On the other end of the phone, Donna says something that makes Henry laugh like a girl.

"Hahaha, yeah, you bet! They're blue as hell. Ha. Anyway, enough about that. Right. Got a pick-up, a sixteen-stone-plus male. You got my GPS?"

Vince watches with bemusement as Henry rocks his head like a pendulum.

"Yep? Okay, that's it, babe. Okay, send the A-Team in, TTFN." He ends the call and grins at Vince. The prick has even had his teeth whitened.

"Who the fucking hell else have you got involved in this now?" Vince says.

"Aubrey Saccharose."

Vince's jaw drops. "Aubrey Saccharose?"

"Yep." Henry is exultant.

"The Aubrey Saccharose of ASBgb Electronics, one of Apple's leading competitors?"

Henry nods.

"The same Aubrey Saccharose who had those allegations of rape made about him last year?"

Henry nods with more enthusiasm. "That's our man."

"Spill."

"Well, to cut an incredibly long and boring story short, Aubes is a sex pest. The allegations were all true. He was unable to control his urges and I may have entrapped him and made him an offer he couldn't refuse."

Henry really is turning out to be a dark horse.

"What did you do?"

"Well, one of our other partners in this, Donna, allowed herself to get in a compromising situation with Mr Saccharose, and I stepped in and told him all about how I could solve all his unwanted urges if he funded our little project."

"And he did all the ritual preps and even..." Vince can't bring himself to say it, so he uses his hands to motion his stomach exploding.

Henry nods but adds, "Although, this is something you obviously don't know yet, not every avatar birth is the same. Christ, from what I heard about Donna's, you don't want to know."

"Donna's?" Vince finds himself caring about someone he's never even heard of.

"Oh yeah, she's one of us. You'll all get to meet each other later today."

"I can't believe this."

"Chill, bro. All you've got to remember is this is all top secret and Aubrey Saccharose will go to any lengths to keep it that way and money is not a problem. Enjoy it, man. Buy yourself some new threads and take that incredibly hot PT out on a date."

Before Vince has a chance to celebrate or protest, the doorbell rings.

Henry shoots a finger at the bolted door. "That'll be the A-Team."

Chapter 30

Henry opens the door and four men in black coveralls come into the place without an invite. Two of them are holding black pistols with laser pointer sights on top of the barrels. Henry points to the door and the two unarmed men unfasten the bolts with no hesitation.

"The tranquillisers we use have enough sedative in them to kill an adult elephant," Henry explains as the pair of armed men enter the room, pistols raised. Vince's avatar is a melancholy heap in the corner of the room, amidst a scattering of paper wrappers with ECOLARD printed on them.

"Shit, why didn't I think of that? Lard! Vince, you're a genius," Henry says, slapping himself on the forehead. "I would've saved loads."

Vince's avatar doesn't look up, pause, or even flinch as two tranquilliser darts stab into its neck, it just chew, chew, chewzzzzzzz and slumps to the floor, pale, greasy, half-melted lard pours from its mouth.

"What happens now?" Vince watches as the four men each take a limb and carry the avatar from the room.

"You'll see."

A Mazda people-carrier driven by someone Vince doesn't see takes him and Henry through town behind an even bigger van. All is black, dark-windowed, and mysterious.

"It's like we're in fucking James Bond, for fuck's sake," Vince says, laughing through the shaded glass at the regular shops.

"It's fucking cool, bro," Henry says.

"Please stop calling me *bro*. You never used to. You can't pretend to be someone you're not just because you don't look like him anymore."

Henry's face falls. "Jesus, man, you're such a fucking killjoy. You should be happy. How much fucking weight you lost so far?"

Vince watches the gym flash past. "Nearly four stone."

"There you go, then. Cheer up, you miserable old bastard. We all have to cut corners at some point in this life."

"I keep telling myself," Sighs Vince, "that if I hadn't done this, I never would have succeeded anyway, but there's still a little part of me that thinks it's wrong."

"Pffff, like fuck is it wrong. And you're right. We would have died fifty-stone whales. What we're doing here is righting an age-old wrong. When that *ancient...whatever the fuck it is*...started sticking its grubby paws into Creation, it left behind some of the most horrendous, vile things humanity is capable of.

Think about it. Alcoholism, drug addiction, sexual deviancy, the desire to kill, even. We have found the way to take away those impulses and lock them away, eradicate that side of us."

"But what do we do with them? The avatars?"

"You'll see," Henry says, and turns away from Vince to stare out of the window.

The cavalcade of two joins the motorway and is on its way north.

Above, in the darkening sky, the comet is like a little pink shuttlecock.

Chapter 31

The black van that leads the way eventually pulls off the motorway onto a smaller road that bleeds into a virtually deserted town. Barely any traffic lines these streets and most of the buildings are in disrepair, shutters clamped shut like crinkled eyelids. Serpentine wraiths stand on corners and secrete themselves in shadowy doorways. The multi-storey car park towards which the van is heading is a charred, godforsaken skeleton covered in decades of insignia.

Vince is sure he's being brought to his death, that this has been an elaborate wind-up, and that before long, one of those guns will be pointed at him and that will be his lot.

They drive through a winding, litter-strewn back street towards the derelict car park. The place is shuttered too, with heavily graffitied doors; as they approach, one of the doors rolls up.

Vince's sense of dread goes into overdrive as the van in front switches off its lights and rolls into the car park. He turns to Henry. "This better not be some kind of Hostel shit where you're going to sell me to some Japanese millionaire to rape and torture, because if it is, I'm taking you with me."

Henry appears hurt but he could be faking. "This needs to be secret, this place has been here a while but has only just become available to us."

The car follows the van into the car park, into total darkness. When they get inside, Vince hears the doors roll back down into place. Lights come on then, regular car park lighting behind rusted wire mesh.

The ground floor of the car park has been used, at some point, as a city for the homeless, evident by the amount of stuff that's been squirreled away under there. Mattresses, blankets, tents, shopping trolleys full of bags. Rodents zip in and out of piles of garbage.

There's a blockade on the ramp leading to the upper floors, consisting of the biggest, most lethal-looking spikes, barbed wire and razor wire that Vince has ever seen.

Red lights flash on as the van ahead turns its lights on and hits the brakes and slows to turn down a descending ramp.

The car park has basement levels. The first sub-ground level is pretty much the same as the ground floor but the headlights immediately pick out another *down* ramp that looks newer.

They drive down it.

"We're here," Henry says once the people carrier has pulled up beside the van. Vince notices three other identical vans parked close by. The men in black coveralls get out, open the back doors, and fire more darts into Vince's avatar before hauling him out and letting him fall.

Waves of disgust then of guilt ring through him as he sees the thing hit the concrete face-first, unable to look away as the front teeth and the nose disintegrate upon impact with the stone.

Henry leaves the people carrier, as does Vince, on legs made of jelly.

Henry walks casually towards a black door in a wall. He presses a button and it slides aside to reveal a lift. He winks at Vince, "They can get the tradesmen's entrance."

The elevator is state-of-the-art, touchscreen everything, chrome and mirrors everywhere. A screen tells them what the weather is like outside as well as showing them complete CCTV footage of the building's perimeters. There are numbers from four down to one; Henry presses three. The lift moves so smoothly it's barely noticeable.

Just in time for the single door to open, Henry says, sounding like a cheesy ringmaster, "Welcome to the freakshow!"

Chapter 32

A small reception area, decorated in grey and black, with just one receptionist: a supermodel in a skirt-suit and headset. Along with an armed security guard, she greets them.

"Hardly a freakshow," Vince murmurs, unimpressed.

"Okay, reception of the freakshow. Hey, Bronwyn, how are you today? I'm sure you've gotten prettier since I last saw you."

The receptionist laughs and flicks her blonde hair. "Oh, Mr Green, you charmer, you."

"Are the others here?"

"Yes, of course, they're in the Green Room as requested."

"Good, good," Henry says, and turns to Vince. "This is our new VIP, Vincent."

The receptionist jumps to attention and stands in a comically provocative pose, tits out, bum out, one-hand-on-one-hip whilst the other reaches forwards over the desk to offer a handshake and an incredibly high-definition view of her expensive cleavage.

"My pleasure, Vincent," she purrs.

Vince hates himself for falling for the obvious facade and hates himself even more for the rapid throbbing in his pants as he clutches her hand.

"Right, now you've met Bronwyn, you can come to meet the partners." Henry shows him into a vast, similarly decorated suite, where one man and two women sit drinking tea and coffee.

They are tainted from the moment Vince sets eyes on them and he wonders what their weaknesses are.

They look normal, but if anyone met Henry today, they would say the same about him.

The man is tall, his long legs stretched out, one crossed over the other as he sips from a cup and scrutinises Vince. Beneath cropped brown hair there are serious eyes, confident, not afraid to make contact with people. He stares at Vince for a few seconds before a shark-grin spreads across his face.

The women aren't as confident as the man; the older of the two has short spiky grey hair and glasses. She looks up at him once and then back down at the contents of her mug. She reminds Vince of one of his primary school teachers.

The other woman has unsettlingly large eyes, they're at least one-and-a-half times bigger than usual, and that's the first thing he notices — that, and her too-long dark brown hair. She's so skinny she's almost waif-like, and Vince instantly finds himself pitying her for some reason.

"Right guys," Henry says, waving at the trio, "this is Vince."

They wave.

"Vince, this is Michael, Donna, and Monique."

Michael nods, the teacher-like lady barely moves, and the bug-eyed stick-insect grins most prettily and says in a common, but not immediately identifiable accent, "Call me *Mon*."

Vince nods to them and sits on a chair Henry is gesturing to. Henry joins them and it's like some kind of AA meeting or being back at the weight clinic. Silence prevails until Henry gets up to go to the hot drinks machine. "Hey, you guys," he calls, like the little girl in The Monster Squad, "tell him your stories."

None of them speak straight away. It's as though they already know each other and Vince is being let into the fold and they're vetting one another's reactions to see what they think of the new recruit. That, or they're mentally deciding who should spill first.

"I was an alcoholic."

Donna is the last one Vince would have bet on talking first. She watches the contents of her coffee cup as she tells. "All day, every day. All my money went on booze. Lost everything, my family, my friends." Donna briefly catches Henry's eye as he comes to sit back down. "When I did the stuff, this idiot suggested I was mostly pissed but I wasn't coerced, I wanted it to stop. I'm glad it's stopped, no matter how much pain I went through having the bloody thing."

"How–?" Vince starts to interrupt.

"Orally," Henry says with a grimace and a hideous, humourless laugh. "Can you imagine that? Giving birth to a fourteen-pound baby orally and your body not having the decency to pass out or die during it?"

"Oh, my fucking God," Vince says, horrified. *I thought I had it bad with my avatar tearing itself away from my abdomen.* "I'm so sorry."

"I can still feel it, hear the noises," Donna moans, "taste its shit in the back of my throat."

"It'll pass, babe, it'll pass," Henry says, with a patronising hand on her knee.

"My story's the same as our Donna's, more or less," Monique starts. Vince thinks her accent is Scottish, proper Irvine Welsh, street-Scottish. "I was on crack from the age of ten and my big brother would pimp me and my sisters out to the estate. It started from there, really. When my avatar made its appearance, I was out of my fucking tree on what would turn out to be my last ever heroin fix."

"Well at least that would have numbed the pain," Vince says, but he can tell from Monique's wry grin that he's way off the mark.

"Ha, ha, I wish. Sobered me right up, that did."

"Oh Christ, dare I ask how you birthed it?"

Monique shudders. "It began as this intense pressure, dead-centre in my head, right behind my nose, between my eyes. That's what brought me out of my high. I couldn't focus, my eyes were all out of sync, boss-eyed or whatever they call it. I felt like I was going to have an epic nosebleed so I leant forward. I was right. Something exploded behind my nose and all this blood gushed out. I thought that would be it but I can feel this lump blocking my sinuses. And it starts to get bigger and I can feel the bones and stuff at the back of my nose and roof of my mouth cracking and —"

"Whoa. Okay, okay, that's enough." Vince's face drops into his hands and he feels pathetic compared to these two women. "I feel like I'm going to puke."

"I was a sex addict." Michael's well-spoken and laughs awkwardly when he announces it. "I was married, had several mistresses, visited prostitutes, and watched copious amounts of pornography. It was all I could think about. It controlled my life. Guess where my baby came out, Vince?"

Vince clamps his hands over his ears and closes his eyes.

"Oh, Henry, I need to talk to you about that thing I mentioned earlier," Michael says, raising his hand like a schoolboy.

Ignoring Michael, Henry stands. "What we have here in this room is five people who are reborn. We have tried all the methods of rehabilitation available to us and failed. This is the only solution left. We are now cured."

"This sounds like a sales pitch," Vince says. "It is, isn't it? You're going to start selling this shit, aren't you?"

Something unspoken passes between Henry and the other three. Donna closes her eyes and shakes her head slowly whilst Michael and Monique grin.

"You're already doing it, aren't you?" Vince asks, already certain he knows the answer.

Chapter 33

The screen shows an overhead of a large room containing a dozen naked figures of all shapes and sizes — all avatars.

"If you look closely," Henry says, freezing and zooming in on one particular avatar, "we've had their other half's initials and dates of birth tattooed on their backs." He presses play.

Pallets of food, nutrition bars of some kind, are stacked against one wall. The whole floor is meshed so anything liquid can be washed away. A water trough runs along one wall, where there are two avatars kneeling over it with their faces submerged. One is being brutally buggered by Michael's avatar as it greedily drinks. Henry points at it. "For the alcoholics."

There are caged avatars hooked up to machinery pumping toxins into them, and another who walks around amongst the Feeders, Drinkers, and Fuckers and routinely slaughters them, waits for them to get back up and start doing their thing again before continuing the never-ending circle.

"It's Hell," Vince declares.

"It's *their* Hell," Henry corrects. "And they enjoy it."

On screen, Michael's avatar cums inside the arse of a drowning white male avatar marked TP230978. Immediately, he pulls out a red-raw penis and looks for another victim. The killer avatar, twice as broad, grabs him by the throat and bashes his head repeatedly against the wall until there's nothing left but pulp. After each kill, the killer avatar, a colossal black woman, roars at the ceiling as if she's bringing down the wrath of God, and gouges thick, stubby thumbs into the nearest avatar's eyeballs. Her victim is a short, plump female Feeder; Vince hates that he's already categorising them. She makes no attempt to retaliate or defend herself and holds on to the chocolate bars in her hands.

"Jesus fucking Christ, who the fuck released that?" Vince shouts.

"Oh, we normally keep our clients strictly confidential but I'll tell you a bit about Betsy."

Betsy's huge hands squeeze the sides of the frumpy Feeder's head and she digs her thumbs deeper.

Luckily, they can't see too much detail, but nevertheless, Vince's stomach still lurches when he sees the barbarian tear the Feeder's head in two. "Who or *what* the fuck is Betsy? It sounds like an abbreviation for a new kind of killing machine."

"Betsy is a larger-than-life, churchgoing housewife who idolises her family, friends, congregation, but has one epic cunt of an abusive husband. She harbours the worst desires to kill. This is extreme passive aggression. She wanted them removed. They're unholy, you see."

"And the husband?" Vince asks, hoping that the embodiment of his abusive urges is running amok in the devil's playground he was witness to.

"Nah," Henry sighs, "he's still a cunt."

Vince turns back to the screen in time to see Betsy's avatar hooking her fingers into another avatar's open mouth and ripping off its lower jaw.

"Okay," Vince says, nauseated, "I think I've seen enough."

Henry switches off the screen. "But don't you see the potential we have here?"

Vince doesn't see potential. He can't see anything other than the carnage he has just witnessed.

"With the success of such franchises as *Saw*, *Hostel*, and now *Squid Game*, there are people, many rich people who would pay to watch this." Henry says, waving at the blank screen, "for entertainment. They are not people, Vince, they are the nasty, festering, persistent little yeast infection that some ancient fucking demon wanked into the primordial fucking soup, man! The Glut jizzed in humanity's mind and his jizz is ever-flowing, Vince, it never ends, every little boy, every little girl is automatically born with the seeds of his greasy, saggy ballbag swimming around in their brains and not all of them can resist those squirmy worms. You couldn't. I couldn't, and neither could those poor wankers, Vince." He nods towards Michael, Donna, and Monique. This is our time to help others like us. So what if the rich get their kicks out of it by betting on demon fights, who cares? They can fund us. They can help us to help others like us."

"Henry," Michael's up with the hand again but Henry shuts him down with a scowled "Later."

Vince sees the passion on Henry's face, tears are pouring down his cheeks, he hammers his fist into his palm like a dictator. With shocking clarity, Vince realises that this is right, Henry is right, and it genuinely shocks him. The other three stare at him in awe and quite rightfully so. Monique looks like she wants to suck his dick so hard he goes back in time.

Henry is right.

Vince moves confidently across to Henry and wraps him in a big bear hug.

"Fuck The Glut!" Vince says, kissing the man on the cheek. "Fuck The Glut!"

Henry hugs him back. "Yes. Fuck The Glut. Fuck The Glut. Let's drain this bastard out of the human race."

Chapter 33

Over the next few hours, Henry shows Vince and the others the facilities at what he calls Project Greenland. The most impressive and thoughtful offering is a birthing suite where all future members partaking in pre-ritual preparations are able to relax in luxury for the last twenty-four hours before their little demons arrive.

There is an executive option, strictly for paying customers, to stay the entire six weeks at the underground site and have full use of the facilities on the adjoining floor: a gym, luxury spa, cinema, and sauna.

Henry insists there will be trained staff to assist clients with their rituals and to offer the necessary anaesthesia for the births.

Vince is impressed by Henry's plans and suggests things that the metalhead has never even considered, such as experimenting on the avatars to see just how they work—and how they might be used for military purposes. Henry is taken aback but glad that he trusted his instinct and let Vince in on the bigger secret.

The five partners separate and go back to their own towns to carry on with their lives.

Henry is the only one who is allowed to recruit new clients for Project Greenland for the foreseeable, but he insists that their roles will come into play very soon.

Chapter 34

Whilst Henry is building his enterprise, Vince focuses on what he can, continuing to shift his weight and become a chiselled Adonis like his friend.

He lives in the gym.

He does everything Nicole tells him to and then some.

They start hanging out together outside the gym.

It starts with him asking her for fashion advice.

"I'm just used to wearing big, bland stuff, not actually ever buying something that I even liked. Always just went for stuff that...well...fit."

They're in a coffee shop, a regular post-gym thing now, and Nicole mentions that his clothes are literally hanging off him with how much weight he's lost.

"Dude, it'll boost your confidence."

"I don't even know what I like," Vince whines.

"I'll come with you. I'll help."

Vince is touched by her offer but still finds the subject of clothing embarrassing. If people know he wears XXXXXL it will confirm his size. "Ah, I don't know."

"We're doing it, and that's that. Besides, I love clothes shopping, and you can give me your opinion on some new outfits."

"Underwear?" Vince risks, adding a chuckle just in case she gets offended.

Nicole rolls her eyes and ignores his question. "Payday. You're having a haircut, too. I know just the place and the perfect cut for you, too. You need to take pride in yourself. You're a handsome man, Vince."

The sun is shining brighter at that moment and he isn't quite sure but he thinks his chin has dropped to the polished floorboards.

"Shut the fuck up, you ugly fucker," Nicole says, blushing and hiding behind her coffee cup. "Jeez, has no one ever given you a compliment before?"

Vince smiles sadly into his own drink, "No. Not really. My mum — when she was still alive — said I had nice eyes."

"How old are you?" Nicole says, his sadness mirrored on her face.

"Thirty-six."

"Now, please tell me to get fucked and mind my own business..."

"Get fucked and mind your own business."

"Ha, ha. Let me finish."

"That's what she said."

"Your mum?"

"Ew. I'll shut up."

Nicole is a woman triumphant. "Right, as I was saying, tell me to get fucked and mind my own business… *shut it*...but, have you ever had a girlfriend before?"

Now it's Vince's turn to blush. He wants to lie, he starts to lie, but the embarrassment cannot be hidden, he's flushing beetroot. The answer he gives is so quiet it's not until Nicole answers that he realises he's said it aloud. "No."

This is it. This is where she is going to ask me out.

Vince tries his best not to let his nerves take over.

"Well," Nicole says, eyes locking on him, "all that's going to change now you're getting super fit and getting a new wardrobe and haircut, isn't it?"

"It is?"

"Totally, dude, women love well-dressed men and I'm sure there are plenty of hot honeys in this town we can find and introduce you to."

"Oh," Vince nods. *Fuck.*

Chapter 35

Nicole's payday comes at the end of the month. Vince is another stone lighter and they are off out for the day. She ushers him into a Turkish barber shop that's right beside the gym and introduces him to a pristinely-dressed man called Mirac.

"Mirac is the best barber in town," Nicole assures Vince as he sits in the barber's chair. "I train him too so he'll give you a discount, won't you, Mirac?"

Mirac looks slightly startled at this news but nods anyhow.

Nicole sits glued to her phone, whilst Mirac attempts to turn Vince's shapeless fuzz into something different and fashionable that will apparently make him look good.

When Vince is in front of the mirror, he realises he hasn't done any posing in front of the mirror since he realised that his successes weren't solely his to celebrate. Food has lost all meaning now; it used to be all he thought about, but now, like the ancient philosopher said, he eats to live, not lives to eat. He's beginning to see the weight he's losing in his face, in the cheekbones and jaw. It's strange, like the sea washing sand off a relic that's never been seen by human beings.

He wonders what he'll look like when he loses as much as he can.

When they get fatter, we get thinner.

Mirac snips and clips and shaves and Vince watches as — miraculously — he does begin to look human.

He doesn't feel human though, he feels like a massive, fat cheater. Others, people at the gym, people at the weight clinic are rooting for him, congratulating him every time they see him, but he knows it's all fake.

I wonder how big he is now?

Vince thinks about his avatar and is almost stricken by a sense of guilt, as if he's abandoned a child, a real child, not a demonic alter ego that had sapped him of willpower all his life and turned him into a gargantuan gonk. Sometimes he's haunted by the images from the avatar room, the collective insanity of it and how docile they all were, apart from Michael and Betsy's avatars, that is, but he's more disgusted at how he took his rage out on his avatar when he kept it prisoner. From what he has seen, it's true that they seem oblivious to pain, can regenerate almost instantly, and even though it's early days, he presumes they will not die until their original host does. There is potential to make millions out of this scheme and he wants to do that with every ounce in his body — but something niggles away: they're missing something, something that's blatantly obvious.

"Hey, that's well sexy," Nicole yells; when Mirac stops fussing with clippers, scissors and combs, she takes a thousand photographs.

Vince doesn't really know whether he likes his haircut or not. It's hard to find yourself when you're nearly forty, and aside from being an over-eater, he is very ordinary.

With mounting horror, Vince realises he's wasted his life, not just by compulsively eating but having absolutely zero interests outside of food.

He tags along with Nicole as they shop for clothes but he doesn't care about any of the things he buys, going along with her suggestions without a second thought. He tries his best to carry on as normal with the banter and jokes, but his PT soon acknowledges that there's something amiss and he spills the beans.

"I don't know what I like."

"What do you mean?"

"Clothes, styles, et cetera."

"Just wear what you like and what you feel comfortable in, those are the only rules."

Vince wishes it was that easy. "I don't have any interests. I mean, I like going to the gym and all this stuff about Frenzel's Comet has ignited an interest in astronomy I never knew I had, but before that, all I ever did was eat, and sit on my arse watching boring telly."

"Mate, you have been reborn. This is the new Vinny 2022, okay? This is your rebirth. It's never too late to start again." Nicole gives him the sweetest, warmest smile and he believes her, buzzes with what she's saying, soaks her positivity like a sponge. Then she ruins it with, "Look at what you've achieved on your own so far!" An image springs to mind of a slightly different, younger version of himself in his spare room, cupping palmfuls of greasy blood and the tip of its own tongue to its mouth.

Chapter 36

Vince opens the group email from Henry and sees that there is a file attached.

Guys,

Take a look at our welcome video, let me know your thoughts,

Henry.

Vince downloads the video and presses play.

Someone who's trying their best to impersonate Morgan Freeman begins the voiceover as a cartoon conveyor belt rolls out from the front of the screen as far as the eye can see.

"In the beginning, when God made Man..."

Identical, featureless humanoids appear on the conveyor and travel along it like they're at an airport. Above them, clouds part to reveal a bright blue sky and a stereotypical caricature of God gazes down serenely.

Vince is instantly reminded of Monty Python and the Holy Grail.

"He made each one individual..."

God's hand comes out of the sky and a big, pointy finger zaps each humanoid, giving each one different features, genders, colours.

A rumbling comes from below the conveyor, a few humans topple like skittles, and a demon tunnels up, most fat and red.

"But the Devil also played a part in the mix..."

The fat demon pricks each person's head with its horns and laughs menacingly. With each person it injects, the demon shrinks until it is virtually non-existent.

"The Devil put The Glut, it's most tempting demon, inside humanity, inside every one of us..."

The cartoon people are civilised now and living their lives.

Some prosper, some fall.

"The Glut is the voice that encourages you to do the wrong thing..."

One cartoon man stabs another.

"Insists that there will never be enough."

A cartoon lady steals food from her children.

"Stops you from saying 'No'."

A pair of cartoon men drink and take drugs.

"Some can resist The Glut's power..."

Athletic cartoon people celebrate victories.

"Others can't..."

An obese cartoon woman waddles down a street for a few steps before keeling over.

"We know that you find this hard to believe, but there is a way to erase this from your mind."

The Morgan Freeman impersonator goes on to explain what is required of everyone before the ritual takes place, every sordid detail, with a cute cartoon accompaniment, as though Henry is trying to sell this to kids.

An animated version of the fat demon from Henry's book appears on screen whilst the cartoon people lay in their bathtubs of yuck and perform their individual rituals.

The fat demon wobbles comically, getting bigger and bigger with each ritual performed.

The video ends.

Nothing is said about the avatars or their births.

Henry,

It's a bag of shit. Are you trying to sell this to children?

Grown-ups, no matter how intelligent, will want scientific jargon. They love scientific jargon.

Whilst I'm fully aware that this particular thing has more than its fair share of tentacles in the supernatural, what is the supernatural but stuff science hasn't scienced yet? That's how I see it, anyway. Show them some before and after photos, blur their faces if you have to if you're worried about confidentiality. You need more evidence, people won't sign up for anything without evidence, you should know that from shit like Weight Watchers and Slimming World.

And why haven't you mentioned the avatars? Surely it's the opportunity to highlight the services Project Greenland offer FOR FREE, you could even introduce some more basic six-week deals for your average Joe that are cheaper than the executive deal.

I think my main point is, don't baby people. Tell them there are disgusting things ahead and that they will suffer intense pain but also tell them they will be amongst trained medical professionals to assist them every step of the way and that the outcome will be euphoric.

Hope this helps,

Vince

He sends the email, sees he's automatically sent it to Michael, Donna and Monique too, but doesn't give that a second thought.

Chapter 37

Henry picks him up in the Mazda the next day without any prior warning.

"You have to come and see this shit," he says, wriggling around like an excited child. "Oh, hey, nice outfit, you boned that PT yet?"

Vince rolls his eyes, cancels his gym session, and goes with his increasingly manic friend.

"Told you the money would come rolling in, didn't I?"

"Yep."

"We've managed to open up three more floors."

"Wait, how many has that place got?"

Henry mimes zipping his mouth.

"So, where's the dosh come from?"

Henry unzips his lips. "The Japanese."

"I knew it would be them."

"I love them freaky bastards," Henry says with a chuckle.

"Isn't that slightly racist?"

Henry shrugs, "Dude, it is what it is — until it isn't."

Vince shakes his head in confusion.

"Anyway, I've...sorry, *we've* made a new contact in said country and engineered a few changes in the name of sport."

Vince stares at him in disbelief. "You're racing the avatars?"

Henry laughs and slaps him on the thigh, "No, silly, we make them fight each other and place bets."

"They were doing that already when I visited two months ago."

"That's true, but things have gotten more organised since then. We've separated them all into individual types, too."

"Really? Categorised them? Well, that's a good idea, I guess, but I reckon Betsy will be pissed off."

"Oh no, she's always busy." Henry reaches into a small fridge and passes Vince a Diet Coke.

Vince opens it and takes a mouthful, and Henry adds, "She's got three hundred cell mates to play with now."

Vince projectiles Diet Coke from his mouth and nostrils.

"Hahaha," Henry says, applauding, "I knew you'd react like that. That's just in the Killer section, too!"

Vince reaches across the van and grabs Henry by his designer tie. "You've got to be fucking kidding me?"

Henry's still laughing, "Nope. We've got loads of the fuckers."

"Stop the van, I'm going to be sick!" Vince leans forward, retching. Henry rubs his back and shouts an order to the unseen driver.

The van immediately pulls over and Vince half-rolls out of the back and pukes up his breakfast. He turns away from the hot slurry of semi-digested porridge he's just slugged up and spots Frenzel's Comet in the morning sky.

If you're going to suddenly spin off-course, now would be a fucking great time.

Henry takes him inside Project Greenland, and as they pass through reception, the first thing he notices is there's a shitload more security, with big guns. Being the pessimist he is, Vince can't help but point out the futility of such weapons if the avatars are untouchable. Un*hurt*able.

"No, but people can," Henry states coldly, "and these babies are specifically designed to knock the avatars out, anyway. I daren't think what would happen if a person got hit with that much sedative. I doubt they'd ever wake up, to be honest. Some of the Killers take a couple of hits."

"Wonderful."

"At least they can be controlled," Henry says, and takes a deep breath. "It's weird, isn't it? Technically, with enough sedation, we could keep them in a coma indefinitely and pump the Feeders, Drinkers and Druggers full of the stuff they need, intravenously."

Oh my God, he's right! "Yes! Let's do that! Why don't we do that instead?"

"But that's just not fun, now, is it?" Henry sounds like every stereotypical movie villain rolled into one. "And not very profitable, either."

Vince sighs and admits to himself that whether he likes it or not, he's in this for the long run. "So where are you taking me?"

"To The Cage."

Chapter 38

The Cage is the size of a football pitch, heavy steel surrounds it on all six sides. An army of armed guards line the outside.

Vince gawps at it and can't help but be amazed at what's hidden beneath this dead town.

Giant floodlights illuminate a canvas flooring, it's like a gigantic wrestling ring.

Large screens show areas of the expanse. Drones fly back and forth to film whatever action goes on below.

Henry and Vince sit in a plus-seated VIP area, they are the only spectators.

"We're still running tests at the moment and I knew you'd jump at the chance to see your baby in action."

"My...?"

"Yeah." Henry points to the screen and Vince sees a comatose pair of figures lying nude, head-to-head in the centre of the cage. One is his avatar.

It has piled on the weight that Vince has lost, fat spreading from the sides of its belly onto the canvas like it's melting. It's aged, too, and its hair has grown into a fuzzy mess and there is a halo of fluff on his face. Vince never could grow a beard. He's nearly caught up with him, by the looks of things. Late-twenties at least.

The other avatar is roughly the same size, completely bald, and at least ten years older.

"I bet you're wondering why they're so clean," Henry says, waggling a finger. "We hose 'em down when we knock 'em out, just in case of germs and stuff." He taps his temple. "See? I think of everything."

"You're all heart."

"They're waking up!" Henry stares intently at the screen, the drones circling above the groggy avatars.

"Hang on," Vince starts, "if they're both Eaters, or Feeders, whatever you want to call them, where's the food?"

"There isn't any." Henry says blankly, not daring to take his eyes from them as they slowly get up. "As I said, this is a test, an experiment. To see what happens."

Vince's avatar pushes itself up to its feet before the other one. It doesn't acknowledge its surroundings, inspecting the immediate area looking for food. The bald avatar does the same and for a second or two they are back-to-back, circling, like something out of Scooby Doo, each oblivious to the other. Vince's starts sniffing the air like a dog and begins to lurch in the direction of the guards. Baldy soon does the same, going to the opposite side of the cage.

"Ha," Vince says, "they won't fight. All they're interested in is food."

Henry ignores him and watches patiently.

When Vince's avatar gets to the side it's salivating, almost rabid. Thick white foam coats its lips. It tries to jump up and catch the buzzing drones but they're too high. It extends an arm through the bars of the cage for the guards but they are out of reach. Baldy is doing the same thing on the other side, it's as if their minds are connected. They push themselves against the metal until skin gives way to bone but they can't reach the men. They stagger back and roar in frustration.

Then they turn and see one another.

"Now it'll get interesting." Henry smiles.

The avatars tear across the canvas towards each other, the only sounds the slapping of feet and the grunts of exertion.

They smash together like two juggernauts in a head-on collision, the recoil sending them both back onto their arses. Baldy is up first and he pounces on Vince's avatar and rips a chunk of flesh out of his neck with his teeth.

"Oh my fucking days, did you see that?" Henry shouts in pure joy.

Vince grabs at his own throat and feels his gorge rise.

Baldy quickly chews the torn morsel and swallows but before he can nip in for another bite, Vince's avatar sits up and clamps his teeth around Baldy's penis and testicles.

"Come on, Vinny!" Vince hears someone shout and realises he's doing it. He's shouting so loud he's made his throat sore.

Henry turns to him and laughs. "I knew you'd get into it. Guess I'm batting for Baldy, then?"

Baldy doesn't react to having most of his genitalia ripped off. Only one of his testicles remains, it dangles on pink gristle, a gory white egg. Vinny appears to find the scrotum and penis more difficult to chew than Baldy did the neck slice and takes a long time to eat. Whilst Vinny is working on his mouthful, Baldy reaches down, grabs both his ears like a football trophy, tears them off, and stuffs them in his mouth.

Vinny bites through the hard testicle and juice squirts across Baldy's thighs. He quickly swallows and darts forward to lick the ball sauce and take a chunk of dough from Baldy's thick leg. Baldy falls on top of Vinny and they begin to roll around in a bizarre, naked, gory cannibal fest. Teeth gnash as they literally eat each other alive. Extremities are the first to go, fingers get nipped off, after nipples and whatever folds of fatty tissue flop in the way.

"This is getting a bit gay," Henry says, after Baldy pulls off Vinny's cock and eats it.

The Original Vince begins to feel weird. Sudden lethargy swathes over him, his skin is too tight, too hot, so are his clothes.

Baldy pushes his hands into a gash he's made in Vinny's guts and tears away a huge flap of fatty belly, he hugs the hunk of meat as he eats and Vinny pathetically gnaws on his foot — he seems to be weakening.

I'm getting fatter. That's what's happening.

Vince's stomach swells and the waistband of his new trousers explodes.

His half-eaten avatar lies in a pool of blood. He sees the bald avatar cramming handfuls of fat like orange caviar into his mouth from a massive slice of belly he's holding. His avatar's belly.

Vince knows what's happening. "Henry!" He shouts.

"Yeah, it's immense, isn't it?" Henry says, without turning around. "I think your avatar's losing, though."

"Henry, stop the fight."

"No, this is fucking awesome. You can't just stop the fight because you're losing." Henry turns and gasps at Vince. "Oh, shit!"

"I'm reabsorbing him!" Vince cries, his clothes splitting.

Henry has the audacity to laugh but he gets his phone out as he does it. Within ten seconds, several of the guards have pumped both avatars full of tranquillisers.

Chapter 39

"Help me, Henry!" Vince screams.

He's strapped to a bariatric stretcher, his clothes are rags. His stomach bulges and extends with unnatural bursts as though bombs are detonating beneath the skin.

Henry jogs alongside the stretcher as guards wheel it from The Cage. He's trying his best not to laugh.

"Is my cock still there?" shouts Vince, prodding beneath his rippling belly. "I can't find it."

"What's new, eh?"

"This isn't fucking funny!" Vince chokes as a roll of fat erupts below his chin.

"You know this reminds me of that Eddie Murphy film, the one where he's a doctor, no, I think he's a professor, yeah, that's right. I think it's called The Mad Scientist or something but he creates this serum to make him skinny and there's this bit where it wears off and he starts ballooning like a cartoo—"

"SHUTTHEFUCKUP!"

Henry flinches like he's been physically slapped by Vince's outburst. He leaves Vince's side and goes to check on the pair of avatars who are being wheeled along, in a stretcher convoy behind.

Vince can feel the cravings come back in floods. He feels ill, lazy, defeated.

He wants it all to stop, to hide away in a supermarket all on his own, and EAT. Chocolate, crisps, bread, butter, cheese, milk, biscuits, *oh fucking God, yeah, biscuits*. To hell with chewing, stick everything in a blender with full-fat cream and blitz it into the richest, most gluttonous gloop that ever existed, and drown in it.

He sees himself fist-fucking gigantic jars of chocolate spread and sucking his brown-caked forearm like a lollipop. He visualises his jaws unhinging, python-like, to consume whole roast chickens, flowed by buckets of gravy and roasted potatoes dripping with goose fat. He climbs up mountains of stuffing and Christmas pudding, the richest of foods, and tunnels into it mouth-first: he's a monstrous mole-rat only built for consumption and defecation.

He burrows deep into the decadent hummock and nestles in the warm moisture within which all he needs to worry about is eating and shitting, eating and shitting, eating and shitting, eating and shitting, eating and shitting.

Eating.

Shitting.

Eating.

Shitting.

Eating.

Shitting.

Eating.

Shitting.

Vince's eyes snap open. There's an oxygen mask on his face.

Henry beams down at him, "Nearly lost you there, bro."

Vince feels like shit. Like a long, soft log. He pulls the oxygen mask off. "How long have I been out?"

"Five years, mate," Henry says, with genuine concern.

"What?!" Vince tries to sit up.

Henry pushes him back down. "No, don't try to get up, we need you to get your rest."

"We?"

"Yeah, me and Nicole got married four years ago, she really lost it when you went into the coma and—"

"WHAT?" Vince swats at Henry's hands but Henry keeps him pinned down. "You fucker, you cunt! You absolute wank-bastard, sugar-coated cuntberg, shit-stained, ostrich-fucker!"

"Wow, Vince!" Henry is clearly impressed.

"I'll fucking cut your fucking bollocks off and sew them to your eyelids and stick your dick down the back of your throat and staple your arsehole to your nose, you — "

Henry's face cracks. "Chill, man, it's only been five minutes, really." Henry presses a button on a keypad and the bed Vince is on adjusts to a sitting position. On the other side of the room, the two half-eaten avatars are surrounded by men in surgical gear. Vince sees his one hooked up to various drips and drains.

"I totally went with that idea I had about feeding them intravenously. I know, I know, I'm a fucking genius. Your matey there is being fed a calorific sugar-and-fat solution that's unbelievably high in everything bad and you'll be pleased to know his regenerative engine, or whatever the fuck it is that makes them heal, has kick-started."

The medics swarming the avatars are giving Vince's the most attention, covering its wounds with thick wads of gauze, just like they would a normal person, and for that he's grateful. The bald one lies unconscious, bleeding from the hole where his genitalia used to be, the lone bollock resting on his bloody thigh. "Why aren't they regenerating properly?"

Henry shrugs, "Fucked if I know, mate, probably something to do with the fact they were eating each other. We'd better not try that again in a hurry. No eating each other." His eyes widen. "Oh, shit. Best find out about Baldy's host. Be right back."

Chapter 40

Vince stays in the hospital room with the two avatars for an hour or so whilst Henry's men patch his avatar up and then Henry comes back into the room with Baldy's twin, his host, strapped to one of those upright gurney things they tied Hannibal Lecter to. "Hey, guys, this is Robert. Robert, this is Vince and the guys."

Robert screams.

Robert is slightly less bulky than his avatar but they're approximately the same age.

Henry has had him stripped. His stomach has raw, red rips where it's expanded much too quickly, blood and fat leaking out.

"Henry, what the living fuck are you doing?" pleads Vince.

"Relax." Henry turns to the medics and a couple of armed guards. "Right, guys, if you could keep a watch on Vince here whilst one of you meds wakes up his avatar, that would be super-duper-pooper-scooper."

Guns point at Vince. One of the medics injects something into his avatar's drip.

"Right, everyone out," Henry shouts and wheels Robert away. His men begin to follow and Vince thinks they're going to leave him in there with his avatar, but they take him too.

In the next room they watch the turn of events.

Vince's avatar, as soon as he's awake, gets off the bed and sinks his teeth into the comatose one still on the bed. It is an arduous but disgusting process.

Vince's avatar peels and pulls and plucks skin, fat, muscle and sinew from Robert's. Pops out his eyeballs with his fingertips and crunches them like pickled onions, tears off his lips, rips out his tongue and swallows it without chewing. Vince's avatar eats with a ferocity Vince has never witnessed before, even in one of his intense emotional binges.

A thick maroon passata oozes from between its buttocks as it bites, chews, slurps and gulps. Robert shrieks in agony as the weight he has lost hits his body as fast as Vince's avatar can eat it off his double. Fat bulges in places where there wasn't any before; it comes back in all the wrong places, his skin splits and stretches to accommodate the sudden extra weight. He piles on three stones in the space of three minutes, all on his stomach.

Vince's avatar keeps going until there's nothing left but bone. It takes hours, but Henry makes them all stay and endure it. And when there is nothing left but the avatar's skeleton, he licks it clean and begins to hammer and claw at the doors for more sustenance.

Robert is a grossly deformed blob. His skin is black-and-purple from burst capillaries, stretch marks, bruises, and burst-open gashes. His moans confirm signs of life but there's not one inch of him that doesn't look as though it's been beaten to a pulp.

Henry takes in the grotesquerie on the upright gurney. "Jesus. State of you, for fuck's sake." He peers into a large fissure on Robert's stomach: internal organs glisten but there's no blood. It could almost be a mutated mouth. Turning to the medics, he says, "Sew him up, will you?"

Henry struts over to Vince and looks kind of sheepish. "So, that's what happens if one avatar completely eats another. Ha. Now we know, eh?"

"You've gone insane!"

"To be honest, mate, I think I've always been a bit bat-shit. But get you, you've gone down at least another two dress sizes, B-friend."

Vince is too horrified, too numb, at the barbarity going on around him to notice the dramatic weight loss he has undertaken in such a short space of time.

"Love to hear how you're going to explain that one to your girlfriend," Henry snorts.

Vince sees his avatar slamming itself against the partitioning door.

It's bigger than he is, now.

Chapter 41

Ah, well. You win some, you lose some.

We'll concentrate on the Killers.

Henry messages Vince and then leaves him in the hands of the medics team after the fiasco with the cage battle and subsequent aftermath.

When the medics have given him the once-over and declared him fit, he is ushered into one of the black fleet vehicles and taken home.

All the way back, Vince slumps against the window, darkness whirring past his vision. Frenzel's Comet is bigger than ever in the sky as it spins round, edging closer and closer.

He's in the shit up to his teeth but he gazes at that piece of space junk and hears Nicole's words in the gym after his first attempt at running.

I bloody well wish on fireworks, mate.

He smiles, but tears come to his eyes.

He wishes on the comet. Wishes for an answer to all this madness.

Chapter 42

Everything is fucked.

He's ruined it.

Michael's fucking ruined it.

The shark-faced ex-sex-addict has fucked the lot of them. Henry says it'll be fine but Vince knows otherwise.

It starts not long after the discovery that if the avatars consume each other, it affects their original hosts.

In the twenty-four hours following Vince leaving Project Greenland he can feel himself, see himself getting thinner, and he contacts Henry to ask why this is happening at such an alarming rate. Henry's men have turned the remains of the bald avatar, who still had brain function, into bone meal and fed it to Vince's avatar.

Robert has now fully re-absorbed his own avatar and reversed the ritual completely. He has made a full recovery and is back to the twenty-eight stones he was at the beginning of his liaisons with Henry and Project Greenland. But Vince's avatar has still eaten, so Vince still loses the fat.

Vince hits the gym, takes muscle building supplements, tries to appear just as confused and surprised as Nicole is at such a drastic weight loss in a short space of time. He puts it down to water retention.

Then the news hits of Michael's betrayal, when he can no longer bleed Henry for money.

The test video, the welcome video that Henry had emailed the four of them, the only ones he'd shared it with, aside from the electrical tycoon Aubrey Saccharose, suddenly appears on YouTube. Making no attempt to keep his identity secret, Michael tells his story, explaining the ritual preparations in the minutest of details.

The real clincher, though, is that he has teamed up with Robert.

Robert tells a heartfelt autobiography of morbid obesity, family loss, the joy of meeting Henry, the disbelief at the ritual of separating The Glut, the hopelessness that makes him want to try anything — no matter how absurd, and then Henry's betrayal. He backs it all up with photographs of himself before, after, and now. There is no infallible proof that these photos were taken in the order they are shown in. There is no proof that the little paper slips from a public weighing machine are in fact Robert's, but that's the beauty, the diseased shotgun effect of all good conspiracy theories: the shrapnel doesn't have to hit everyone, just enough to infect and help spread the contagion.

It works.

Vince acts dumb to it but everyone in the gym is on about the latest whacko theory on the internet. The majority of the population think it's totally nuts, have nicknamed the believers *Glutters*. Even those who believe there's even the slightest possibility. Vince laughs along with them and tries his best to pile on as much muscle as possible but that isn't an easy thing to do.

Glutters start showing themselves on the street. They're proud of their devotion to total abstinence of personal hygiene, embracing it and wearing their filth like battle scars. After all, they've been given something to believe in, proof that life goes on, that all their wrongdoing isn't their fault.

Normal folk shun them, as is only to be expected; these delusional people are in various stages of a six-week period of complete degradation.

The world stinks. Even more than usual.

Chapter 43

This is what happens to people who betray me. I advise you all to watch these videos. If any of these get out, you will all suffer similar fates.

The email is from Henry and comes complete with two video attachments. It's been sent to Vince, Donna, and Monique; one is labelled *Michael*, the other *Robert*.

He really doesn't want to, but Vince presses play.

Back to the drones in the caged arena.

Off-screen, the sound of a man screaming blue murder.

The cameras show four guards dragging Michael kicking and screaming towards The Cage's entrance. He's giving it his all, using every bit of fight he has in him to get away, biting at them when he can't move anything else.

"Please," he begs, "PLEASE! Henry, please, I'm sorry!"

A drone circles overhead and captures the struggle beautifully. Michael shrieks up at it like a religious martyr beseeching their god for an end to their suffering. "Henry!"

The guards throw him through the heavy iron gate and onto the canvas. Michael falls and rolls — he's only in t-shirt and jeans—and as a drone swoops in for a close-up, his forearms are red raw from the force of the impact.

He's up in an instant, immediately scouting the football-pitch-sized area for whatever is obviously going to attack him.

Whoever is controlling the drones and the rest of the cameras allows a few long seconds to pan out and shows that aside from Michael, The Cage is empty. Michael frowns and then laughs in disbelief, then tears of relief begin to surface in the corner of his eyes.

"Okay, okay, consider me warned," he shouts to the deserted square in the hope that Henry is listening. "I have actually pissed myself." He points to a darkening patch on the crotch of his jeans. "I'm sorry, okay. I get it. I'll make it up to you."

The camera zooms in on Michael's smiling face as it slowly turns upward and something wet lands across his lips and nose. The smile is gone and replaced with absolute trepidation.

Michael bolts away quicker than the cameras can keep up with.

Another angle change shows a man-sized mesh coffin being lowered into The Cage.

Masturbating as fast as his arms will allow, is Michael's avatar. The bulbous tip of its penis is squeezed between the wire, its fat, bulging testicles mashed against the grid adding extra sensation.

As the coffin touches down, another thick, translucent stream of sperm shoots out of its dick and the box opens.

Michael is already at the opposite edge of The Cage.

A drone catches up with him and shows him six feet off the floor, climbing up the walls like a monkey.

Michael's avatar caresses his swollen nuts with one hand, rolls them together like Chinese Baoding balls as he scans the horizon for something to love. He spots something living, flesh-and-blood and warm and tight. He lets out a tribal war cry and runs across the open plain to capture his prey, his long, hard prick an angry purple spear.

Drones come to map Michael's ascent and he bats them away as if he's King Kong. He risks a glance over his shoulder and sees his avatar tearing across the canvas.

He climbs higher.

One of the drones gets too close and Michael snatches it from the air, another shows him smashing it against the metal bars and wielding it to see if it could form a makeshift weapon.

He's not even halfway up The Cage side and his avatar has already started to climb.

Aiming for his avatar, Michael drops the dead drone but misses completely. He climbs faster and then he slips and is hanging by just one hand.

The drones swoop in to show the expression of pain on his face and how it quickly turns to one of defeat.

Michael lets go.

The camera quickly changes to show the depth of the drop. Michael falls; his avatar reaches out pathetically as he passes him, and hits the floor.

Miraculously, Michael is still alive. His legs are an explosion of blood and splintered bone and he screams with the blinding white agony of it all.

His avatar drops like a ballerina behind him but still Michael doesn't give up. Using his hands, he drags himself away from his double, managing a few feet before his avatar is on him.

The avatar reaches down between Michael's legs and rips the arse out of his jeans and underwear. It grabs the man's buttocks and tears them apart whilst simultaneously thrusting.

Michael screams as he feels what is technically his own erection rammed up his arse with no lubricant. His avatar grinds his face into the canvas as it goes at him like a pneumatic drill.

Trying to push himself up so he can breathe, he spits a mouthful of blood and teeth. The avatar grunts and yanks out his livid, vermilion-wet member and grabs Michael by the ears.

Michael feebly rains punches at the avatar, at its genitals, stomach, anything, but it's no use, it feels no pain. They feel no pain.

It drives its dick into Michael's ruined mouth and it lands its own punches to the sides of Michael's head as it skullfucks him. Glorious technicolour shows the exact moment Michael's jaw shatters and geysers of grisly guy-gunk gush from his nostrils and land on his twin's twitching, emptying bollocks. Michael's a wretched thing on the floor, a broken and bloody rag doll.

Still frantic with rape, his avatar pulls away his remaining clothes and grips the root of Michael's penis and the sack housing his testicles. Without making a sound, his avatar yanks them off and throws them into the air with a triumphant grin.

Michael pales rapidly as blood spurts from his crotch and death approaches.

His avatar smears crimson up and down the shaft of his penis and over his balls and kneels. He's slow and gentle as he carefully eases himself into the new hole he's made. The avatar looks deep into Michael's fading eyes and fucks the life out of him.

Michael is immobile and quite obviously dead, but his avatar repositions him to begin again with anal penetration but stops short with an out-of-the-blue burst of what is clearly humanity, and recoils from the dead body. He backs away on his haunches, the cameras showing something startling on the avatar's face - emotion. Horror, confusion, and maybe more than a little wonder.

It's been reborn with a blank, but complete mind: it's human.

Across The Cage, gates open, guns cock.

The once-avatar looks inquisitive at the strange figures approaching, begins to stand, but before it fully rises, it's riddled with bullets.

It falls down.

It doesn't regenerate.

It doesn't get back up.

Chapter 44

Vince forces himself to watch Robert's video.

Back to The Cage.

It contains around fifty Feeders of all shapes, sizes, ages and genders.

Every Feeder has something strapped to their naked backs, something that keeps Vince's attention. They're containers to hold a certain number of the bars they are fed on. The Feeders take from each other and stand eating, docile, like cows. Vince knows the containers will only hold enough to keep them busy for a few minutes, judging by how quickly they eat.

Similar to Michael's punishment, a smaller overhead cage is used, except this time, Robert is inside it. Vince is thinking about the guy in Jaws when Robert is lowered slowly over the mass of Feeders.

As their food runs out, they immediately smell the new source and reach and jump to try to be the first to grab a taste.

It must be a natural reaction as Robert tries to climb the insides of the small box he's in, even though he's exposed all around.

The avatars swarm the coffin as soon as it's within their grasp; one more lithe avatar scrambles up the outside of the cage and stretches into its confines.

Robert cries out as the avatar's long fingernails dig into the wide roll of fat around his gut. He thumps at its hand and manages to back away, against another side. Teeth sink into the soft white flesh that spills through the cage and a chunk of Robert's buttock is torn away with ravenous hunger. He screams out in pain and is buffered from side to side as all around the cage, hands dart in to rake, pinch, grab, and take his flesh.

Robert and the mesh coffin vanish beneath a writhing mass of overweight, multicoloured flesh. They soon topple it and a number of the avatars' arms are crushed. The noises Robert makes are like nothing Vince has ever heard; every time he surfaces above the reeling meat sea there is a little bit less of him.

They're piranhas with hands. Vince sees one reach in and grab the top of Robert's head and a drone zooms to capture what is suspected to be quality viewing. Grisly fingers scrunch in Robert's sweat and his blood-soaked hair, others find the soft parts of his face, his eyes, cheeks, lips, his double chin, and pull and peel and pluck and tear.

Vince turns away when dark brown claws with yellowed nails sink into Robert's tongue and yank it from its moorings. He ends the video as the avatars begin to participate in a tug o' war with Robert's corpse.

Henry is insane, a homicidal maniac with clearly more than one of The Glut's slick tendrils in his head. There is nothing he can do now apart from see this through to the end.

Chapter 45

The streets are lined with filthy Glutters in various stages of verminous decrepitude. They gather together, dishevelled; they would be mistaken for street people if not for the home-made placards they carry advertising the reasons for their own defilement.

I BELIEVE IN THE GLUT.

RELEASE YOURSELF.

FREE YOURSELF FROM YOUR URGES.

IT'S NOT YOUR FAULT.

SEVER THE GLUT!

CUT HIS TIES.

FREE YOURSELF!

The slogans are endless, and there seem to be more and more of them every day.

Beneath the ever-prominent comet in the sky, the world looks pre-apocalyptic.

Vince goes to the gym, tries to carry on with life as normal, but there's a group of the smelly bastards on the high street arguing with some of the street preachers.

Up until now, the Glutters have been peaceful, but things always get heated when arguments are had with conspiracy theorists and neither the Glutters nor the Christians have any valuable proof to show one another.

A white-haired old man, one who is usually spreading God's word outside Poundland, has a bearded Glutter by the throat up against the kebab takeaway. They shriek at each other whilst the two workers, Vince's acquaintances, stare goggle-eyed beneath their badly-spelled menus.

The Glutter thwacks the religious nut with his placard and a scuffle ensues.

Dirty people with bad habits they can't quit have half-hearted battles with people who are just as corrupt on the inside as they are on the out.

They all think they're right.

Police sirens wail, lights flash.

Vince goes to the gym.

"It's madness out there," Nicole says. She's watching similar gatherings and altercations on the news. "I'm glad you're not a raving loony, mate."

He can hardly bring himself to speak to her, the guilt is so high. He says nothing and goes to the changing room.

"Hey, you alright?" she says, when he comes back out to find her.

"Yeah, just a little out of it today, what with all that shit out there. I can't believe so many people are believing in this stuff."

"It's fucking bollocks."

Vince nods.

"You got plans tonight?" Nicole changes the subject as they head over to the weight section.

"Since when do I ever have plans?" Vince jokes.

"You should sign up to one of these dating sites."

"Fuck that, I'd rather meet someone in person. That way, they can see what they're getting into straight away."

Nicole shrugs but agrees. "Well, I'm taking you out, then. My treat. It's a surprise, a reward for you losing eight bloody stones, you awesome bastard."

Vince is touched, but his guilt only worsens. "Actually, it's nearly nine, now."

Nicole gawps at him. "You are a fucking legend, mate, honestly. I owe you."

"How do you owe me?"

"Dude, people have seen your success and for some crazy reason think I have something to do with it — "

"You do, you — "

"No, it's all you," Nicole insists, and pokes him in his newly forming pecs. "All you, sweetheart. Your hard work, your blood, sweat and tears. Your willpower."

Vince feels like absolute shit. Somehow, he gets through the gym session without crying.

Chapter 46

Vince walks home aching; a couple of the regular town Glutters are suddenly clean and he knows perfectly well what that means. They've performed the degrading ritual.

He feels nauseated at recalling stepping into that tepid bathful. Part of him wants to tell them about what's to come but a bigger part is worried about the consequences.

His phone pings: it's his weekly allowance from Henry. It's increased since Michael's demise and he can only surmise it's the ex-sex-addict's wages split.

Vince tries to force himself to be happy.

Henry insists that he and the elusive Aubrey Saccharose have the current fiasco in hand, that they will right Michael and Robert's sabotage, but even if they do, Vince questions his morals about whether the whole bloody facade is the right thing or not.

No matter how you look at it, it's cheating, and one thing that his parents always used to drum into him as a child was: *cheaters never prosper*.

There's a message from Nicole reminding him she's picking him up at seven-thirty and to dress smart-casual.

He gets ready with two hours to spare, and must tell her the truth tonight. That he is a Glutter, one of the first, and that all this hard work would not have been possible in the first place if he had been the man he was before he found out the answer to Henry's weight-loss riddle. The old Vince never even looked at the gym when he passed it, let alone entertained the idea of actually using it. If the old Vince, by some preternatural turn of events, stumbled into the gym and began to use a piece of exercise equipment, he would have given up within seconds, never again to set foot on the unhallowed ground. At least if he's honest with Nicole, it will hopefully ease some of that guilt.

A loud, metallic crash rouses him from his reverie and he rushes to his window.

There's a car crashed through a bus shelter; the driver is clawing at his face. A crowd of people rush to his aid.

Vince goes outside to see if he can help.

Someone's already ringing for an ambulance and everyone else who checks to see if the driver is okay recoils from the vehicle.

Vince can handle anything after the things he's seen.

He pushes past the onlookers and sees what they've been grimacing about.

The driver has something embedded in the side of his head and is smacking his hand at it.

"Stop," Vince yells.

The poor bloke's obviously smashed his head open; his shaven dome resembles a blood-filled cracked boiled egg.

Then Vince notices the blood spilling down over a deep cleavage and a heavy pair of breasts. It's coming out of the side of her head. People scream as an angry red baby face fractures and completely obliterates the woman's ear and pushes its head out through her earhole.

Through the closed window, Vince hears the lady's skull cracking. Blood and bone splatter the glass. He blocks the view from the other onlookers as half the woman's head concaves and a baby fist bashes a hole through the top of her skull. She is somehow still alive, awake and aware. Pressure from the sprouting baby breaks her neck and she slumps forward, her seatbelt preventing her hitting the steering wheel.

Across the street, there's another horrendous screech.

Another shaven-headed person is doubled over and holding their buttocks together as something implodes or explodes and the seat of their trousers stains red.

The births have begun.

"Sorry I'm late, I think there was an accident or something," Nicole says as she parks up behind

Vince's flat in a surprising choice of vehicle, a bright red, double-cab pickup truck. It's immense.

"This is your car?"

"Nah, mate, stole it on the way, didn't I?" Nicole rolls her eyes.

"I was expecting something I'd have to shoehorn myself into."

"I like big trucks—"

"—And you cannot lie?"

Nicole smirks at him, it makes him temporarily feel good and forget what he's just witnessed.

He doesn't know what she has planned tonight but with what he's seen and what he knows, he can tell that the shit is going to hit the fan in a way mankind has never known before. This may be his last chance at normality for a long time.

Nicole takes him to a pub. It's quiet here—and dare he think it, romantic. There's a heated veranda and they share one of the cosy little glass capsules that cropped up in the better of the beer gardens and outside eateries everywhere during the pandemic.

"Have whatever you want, mate," Nicole says, handing him a menu. "You've bloody well earned it, and besides, I'll make you burn it off later." He looks up at her with a start and she cracks up. "At the gym, you dirty old pervert!"

Vince feels himself redden. He takes the menu and scans it immediately, looking for the healthiest options.

Nicole catches him. "Mate, I'm having a mixed fucking grill with all the trimmings. Have. What. You. Want."

But Vince can't. He can't have what he knows is inherently bad for him, what his brain tells him is unhealthy. It's been this way since he separated from his avatar, since the ritual. The mere thought of eating something that his brain says *no* to makes him feel like throwing up.

"I really want this," Vince says, pointing to what is quite possibly the blandest option on the menu.

Nicole scrutinises him for a long, hard couple of seconds before her face lights up. "You and your iron will. I'm so proud, but prawn salad is the gayest thing I've ever known a man to eat. Just saying. Sure I can't tempt you to chuck a steak on there?"

Vince shakes his head and smiles. "I'm sure what you're having is heterosexual enough for both of us."

"Too motherflipping right, mate." She jumps up and runs inside the pub to order. Vince bangs his head repeatedly against the capsule wall.

Frenzel's Comet is an inch above the horizon now; it'll be gone from the skies soon, venturing into deeper space to bypass other wonders. Vince wishes he could strap a saddle to it and ride along.

Chapter 47

Dinner's great; he genuinely enjoys what the old Vince would have called rabbit food and is truly amazed at how much Nicole can put away. "You're like the Tardis."

Nicole laughs through a mouthful of beer-battered onion rings. "Are you a Doctor Who fan?"

"I used to be, up until a few years back."

"Oh, right, who put you off? Let me guess, Matt Smith? Capaldi? Don't tell me it was Tennant. If you tell me it was David Tennant, I'll swear to God I will walk away from this table right now!"

"Sylvester McCoy," Vince mumbles into his drink.

"Who?"

He says it louder, clearer, and Nicole is gobsmacked. "Dude, you have to get over that eighties shit! You need to catch up."

Vince pulls a face and Nicole bounces up and down in her seat. "Right, mister. Me and you are going to watch Doctor Who until you are up-to-date."

Vince doesn't mind having to spend more time with Nicole but he will have to tell her his secret; if she still wants to be his friend afterwards, then he will happily watch all the sci-fi she wants him to. "Okay, there's just something I have to tell you first—"

"Hold that thought," Nicole interrupts, "I'm going to get dessert." She darts back into the pub.

Dread froths up inside of him as he sees a waiter approach their table with an ice cream sundae that's overflowing with sauce, cream, and chocolate. It's so big it dominates the tray that he holds aloft at shoulder height. As he places the tray down, he reveals a beautiful fruit platter, too, and Vince is truly touched when the waiter doesn't make a big deal about giving the healthy stuff to the fatty.

" Vince spies at least twelve different types of beautifully prepared fruit. "Wow!"

Nicole dives into Mount Sundae. "Doesn't it even bother you now?" she asks, creamily.

If only you knew. Vince shakes his head and avoids concentrating on the gluttonous mulch that she's virtually inhaling. He doesn't want to lie to her anymore; he's plucking up the nerve to tell her. "If I could trust myself to moderate, then I could eat anything—but I know if I eat something bad it'll open a Pandora's Box that will be nigh-on impossible to close. Normal people—"

"Who's normal?"

"Well, I take it you don't usually eat like you have done tonight, otherwise you wouldn't be so fit."

Nicole nods. "Special occasions, birthdays and stuff. But this sort of thing is supposed to be a treat. Treats aren't an everyday occurrence, they're to be earned."

"Exactly," Vince says, "with me, with how I used to be, every occasion was a reason to overindulge like this but normal people, like you, can turn it on and turn it off like a tap without, and correct me if I'm wrong here, any guilt. I can't take that risk again. It's probably like alcoholism or drug abuse, just once is enough to fuck everything up." Vince is close to tears now but doesn't care, he's ready to tell her what he did, that he took part in the ritual, that he extracted the gluttony from his brain. He sobs. "Food, in the wrong mind, is a drug."

Nicole is beside him, arms wrapped around his shoulders, and he cries like a baby — and still he hasn't told her. She comforts and holds him and soothes him; even a bird's-eye view down her amazing cleavage doesn't stop the tears coming. He wants to tell her, needs to tell her, tries to tell her, but she stems the flow of teardrops by thrusting a tartan-wrapped package into his hand.

"What's this?" Vince says, weepy.

Nicole blushes, backs off, retreats coyly to her dessert. "Open it."

Vince's hands shake as he unwraps the oblong package to reveal a dark-brown leather box with a golden clasp. He unlatches it and inside is a brass telescope that gleams beneath the outside lighting. He's speechless.

Nicole sneaks a look over her right shoulder. "Tonight, and tomorrow are the last two nights we'll be able to see your comet."

Vince sits, mouth agape.

"You look like a goldfish," Laughs Nicole.

Vince laughs a little, but there are still tears.

Chapter 48

They've parked up on Boxford Tor, a great spot for stargazing. Nicole's set them up somewhere comfy to sit in the back of her pickup and Vince insists she be the first to use the telescope. "I never realised stars were so beautiful," she says.

He loves the child-like wonder on her face and regrets every lewd thought he's ever had about her.

"Point me in the direction of this comet."

Vince carefully moves the telescope, it's ice-cold to the touch, towards the Roman candle in the heavens. "Oh my God, mate, it's prettier than anything I've ever seen...and so red."

Vince grins like an idiot, happy that they're sharing this perfect moment.

"Here." Nicole passes him the eyeglass and he brings it up to his eye but keeps it closed to make the anticipation last even longer.

The astronomers haven't predicted when Frenzel's Comet will come by this way again, they've not mapped its trajectory satisfactorily enough to decide that yet. It could be another Halley's and return every seventy-five years but the theory is that this is a once-in-a-lifetime opportunity, not just anyone's lifetime, either, but only those who are alive to see it now. Who knows when this fantastical ball of stardust will return?

Vince takes a deep breath in and out, feeling the newly-strengthened muscles in his chest and abdomen rise and fall.

Everything will be alright, a voice like his own tells him. Henry will sort this mess out, he has the manpower, and Nicole will understand. She's intelligent. *Everything. Will. Be. Alright.*

He opens his eye and a lancing pain rips up his insides, vomit explodes from his mouth and nose and a dark liquid voice, older than the stars, chuckles in his head and says, **LIKE FUCK IT WILL**.

He drops the telescope on the bed of the pickup and hears the glass shatter amongst the puddle of puke. The afterimage from the red light burns in his left eye, he hyperventilates and heaves up the rest of his dinner.

"Oh my God!" Nicole's hands flutter to his spasming back, he grips the truck's sides as dizziness overwhelms him. Whatever is ailing him is determined to see him fail. His arms go numb, the words *heart attack* flash across the blind spot in his left eye, and he face-plants his upchuck.

It all comes back to him, the surreal astral trip he'd experienced and had completely forgotten about. Floating in space over a sickly red star. Then landing on black rock which scorched his skin and that thing, that gigantic thing that was all belly, fat, grease and mouth.

Oh, God.

Sensation flows back into his arms.

He's covered in regurgitated prawn salad and a dozen different fruits. He pushes himself up onto his elbows.

Vince knows what that thing is in the sky.

It's not a comet. It never has been.

It's The Glut — and it's coming for them. Coming for them all.

When he realises he is screaming, he stops and stares in fear at Nicole, who seems equally terrified. "Bad prawn, I think."

Chapter 48

"What's with all the blues and twos?" Nicole's face is scrunched up with concern as she watches a trio of ambulances and a pair of police cars pass her.

"God knows," Vince mumbles and tries to call Henry again. For the ninth time, Henry doesn't pick up, this only exacerbates his anxiety.

"You sure you're okay?" Nicole takes her eyes off the road to give him a brief look of concern.

"I'm fine," Vince insists, terrified. "I'm sorry about the mess."

"Don't worry about it, it usually gets really muddy anyway, what with some of the boot camps and stuff I set up outside. I'll just hose it out before I go to bed."

Fear is paramount in Vince's mind, everything feels like it's over, he wants to at least show Nicole that he has been grateful for all her help. "Look, I'm really touched by your gestures tonight, no one's ever done anything so sweet for me. I'm sorry I dropped the telescope—"

"Oh, chill, it only cost a tenner off Wish anyway."

Vince can't help but feel a smidgen of disappointment. "I'm just really grateful, and for all the help you've given me over the last few months."

He pauses, looks up to the cab's interior to find the right words, or even the wrong ones.

"There's something I need to tell you, Nicole—"

"I'm going to let you fuck me." Nicole interrupts Vince with a jaw-dropping whammy.

Vince is so glad he's not the one driving; if he were, he would have probably been responsible for a twenty-car pile-up. All thoughts of the evil entity in the sky are temporarily vanquished as he shouts, "What?"

Nicole squeezes his inner thigh and flashes him a smile. "I really like you, Vince. I admire you. I really want to be your first."

Vince is agape.

"You're goldfishing again," Nicole smirks. "What's the matter?"

"WHAAAAAAAAAAAT?"

"Don't you want to?" Nicole is taken aback, shocked even, as though she'd never guessed that *no* was an option.

Vince forces out words. Slowly. "You're like five years younger than me."

Nicole shrugs. "It's just sex, it doesn't have to be a big deal."

"Doesn't have to be a big deal?" Vince exclaims, "that's the thing though, I don't think I'm capable of doing something like that and it not being a big deal."

"Mate, I really like you, and I love hanging out with you, so why don't we take it slowly from there?"

Vince's hormones take control of his brain for a moment and remind him that the world could quite possibly be ending very soon by the arrival of a monstrous fat demon. They also take control of his voice box. "But immediate sex first, yeah?"

Nicole cackles, "Let's go test your bed out."

Nicole's kissing him as soon as they get into his flat and he's so turned on he honestly thinks he'll shoot in his jeans and ruin everything. His phone starts vibrating like a motherfucker in his trouser pocket and that really isn't helping matters. He pulls it out — Henry picks his fucking moments — and throws it on the nearest chair. Nicole asks where the bedroom is and he points to it worriedly.

He doesn't know what state it's in, *I'm a single man, for fuck's sake, there might be dirty pants in there, cum-socks, anything.*

She kicks off her shoes and darts inside, laughing excitedly.

Vince follows as fast as he can and he feels like he's ninety percent cock even though it's barely five inches in reality.

Nicole is standing on his bed and she's already in just her underwear and Vince knows just by this gorgeous sight alone he'll be lucky if it even gets inside her.

"Oh, Jesus fucking Christ!" He wheezes as she unhooks her bra. He feels like he's going to have a coronary.

A last-minute bout of confidence issues rears its ugly head and in a way it's his hero, cooling him off a bit as he worries about taking his clothes off in front of someone so perfect.

Nicole steps off the bed and her hands do it for him — and against all odds, she's smiling. "Lie down."

Vince does as he's told, tries his best to regulate his breathing as they are both now in their underwear. Nicole sits across his thighs and removes her last remaining item of clothing and pulls down his boxer shorts.

As soon as the air hits his erection, he's sure it's going to go off.

Nicole must sense just how nervous and aroused he is. She doesn't hesitate. She grabs his hands and forces them to grab hold of her breasts and lowers herself onto his dick.

It's the best ten seconds of his life and when it's over, Nicole smiles and says that she's going to be giving him lots of private PT sessions to teach him everything there is to know.

They lie in each other's arms for ages: he ignores his phone vibrating, ignores the outside world, ignores everything else — he suspects, just like his one and only sexual encounter, that it will all end too soon.

Chapter 49

"Where did you get this?"

Vince wakes up and Nicole is standing beside the bed doing the stereotypical girlfriend thing and wearing one of his t-shirts. She looks livid but is still sexy as fuck. There's a sheet of paper in her hand. The photocopy of the ritual details.

Shit! I thought I'd binned that! Vince's immediate reaction is to lie, tell her he downloaded it from the Internet and considered becoming a Glutter. Words refuse to come out; as Nicole would say, he's goldfishing.

"Why did you go through my bag?" She asks, hurt. "Why?"

"Huh? I didn't."

Vince is now genuinely clueless and thinks he must have misheard her.

Without warning, Nicole bursts into tears and slumps onto the bed.

"I'm sorry." Vince spits the words out, not vehemently, it's just that they're hard to say. "I was going to tell you. I didn't want you to be disappointed in me."

She glares at him, "What, that you're a thief? Were you trying to get some of your gym session money back after fucking me?"

"Huh? What the fuck are you on about? I'm not a thief."

"So, what were you doing going through my bag, then? Need a fucking tampon to stick up your fucking arsehole?"

Vince stifles a laugh, "No, I didn't go through your ba—"

"Wait!" Nicole lifts the sheet of paper and her fingers flutter by her mouth. "This is yours, isn't it?"

"Well, duh!" Vince says, rolling his eyes.

"Ah."

"Wait…" Vince is slow to catch on and when he does it's super-duper, mega goldfish time with added pointy fingers. "You thought it was yours!"

Nicole laughs and averts her eyes. "Yeah, I think we need to talk."

Hot drinks or booze are a must for any deep and meaningful conversation and as Vince is currently in charge of his own health and never been a drinker, coffee is on the table.

They sit in silence for a few minutes, each waiting for the other to start.

Vince wants to do the right thing before it's too late to do anything.

"I always fail. I always tried, but I always failed almost immediately. I never had the fight inside me. The older I got, the more detached from other people I became. Food was the only thing I found comfort in. I felt like the only way I'd ever conquer this would be if someone possessed me or I had my brain rewired."

"Ditto," Nicole says quietly.

"What?"

"What? You don't think I had the same issues as you?"

"Not unless you found out about this shit years before me!"

"I was a binge-eater. I'd starve myself for as long as I could and then I'd go mental, tear through a family-sized birthday cake in two minutes, and then I'd force these two fingers," she holds them up, "down the back of my throat and throw it all up. It's called bulimia, Vince. Not just you fatties that have eating disorders."

Goldfish.

Nicole reaches across the table and grabs his hand. "But this is good. We've got even more of a bond now. And that shit in our heads was killing us. What's left, what's left is all *us*, mate! We've done everything since, this is pure us, undiluted us, without any demon-shit infecting our brains. It's almost like we've evolved, man."

"I never saw it like that. I thought I was cheating."

Nicole laughs. "You think medicines are cheating? Public transport is cheating? It's not, you've just cured yourself. Jesus, you're such an idiot."

Vince laughs, a great weight having been lifted from his shoulders. "It doesn't bother you?"

Nicole shakes her head and kisses him. "It makes me want to be with you even *more*. We have a connection, we've been through similar shit," she pauses to pull a disgusted face, "quite literally."

Vince smiles the biggest smile he's ever smiled.

"Where do you keep yours?"

"My what?" Vince is back to being confused again.

"Your double."

"Oh fuck," Vince says, and headbutts the table.

Chapter 50

Vince briefly looks at his phone as it vibrates on the chair, the caller I.D is Henry's. Yet again he ignores it: everything is going to the dogs but it's more important for him to get things straight with Nicole.

"Tell me, who got you into this?"

"My mum."

"Your mum?"

Nicole nods. "She had this toyboy, ten years younger than her. I didn't like him much. They met at some rock club. She was overweight by about six stone but he was a fucking mountain. He was into all this dark metal shit, the scary black stuff where they supposedly do blood rituals and sick things. It was him who found this old book at the digs of an acquaintance of his."

Vince had a sinking feeling that he knew who this man was.

"His acquaintance was like this Satanic librarian, reckoned he had the world's most dangerous books," she says, rolling her eyes at repeating the words of a braggart. "My mum's bloke found this book all about us, humans, and how there really is no such thing as one true god. We are all just tools used to feed these immortal beings outside of our own universe. We're like the little cheese wheels in Trivial Pursuit and each one of these ethereal deities has its own cheesy wedge in us. Different things we do feed different ones, even the so-called good things." She gives a hollow laugh. "Fucking depressing, or what?"

"Jesus."

"But this book teaches you how to separate yourself from these beings, so that must mean that there is something that's just ours left."

"The cheese holder."

"Yeah," Nicole laughs, "the cheese holder."

"So, mankind won't be released from these things' binds until he has learned how to free the cheese?" Vince tries not to smirk, he's actually scared – and that only makes things worse.

"Yes. My mum's boyfriend stole one of the pages from the section that mostly dealt with freeing the cheese that makes us do things that are detrimental to our health that we don't seem to have control over."

"What was his name?"

Nicole shrugs, "I don't know, but he was a big bastard with black hair and a beard."

"Henry?"

"It might have been, yeah. Why?"

"I'll tell you when you've finished."

"Okay, well my mum ups and leaves me and does everything that it says to do on the page along with her bloke. Then she comes back home with no hair, a totally different temperament, and has another her with her."

"Her double?"

"Yeah. I thought she was going to spill some family beans about having a long-lost twin but she's honest from the start. The double is the part of her that made her fat, that ate away at everything, including her willpower. It constantly needed to be fed, like twenty-four seven, and even though I worked extra hours at the gym to help her out, she couldn't afford to feed it."

"What happened?"

"She kept spending more and more time on her own with it and every time she came out of the room, she looked drained, like she'd had the life drained out of her. She began losing weight at an impossible speed, her skin hung from her bones until she looked like she was melting. It was sucking the fat and muscle out of her somehow. It killed her and ate her." Nicole started crying. "I didn't know what to do. I came home one day and it was like I'd dreamt everything. Mum was back the way she was, fat and unhappy. She killed herself whilst I was at work."

"Oh my God."

"You want to know the best of it?" Without waiting for him to answer, Nicole continues, "She left me thousands in her will. Thousands she could have spent to feed that fucking thing."

"Why...why the fuck did you do it? After seeing what happened to your mum?"

Nicole's face darkens to red anger. "Because I saw her boyfriend looking fit as fuck, that's why. He bloody well succeeded."

Vince slams his fist on the table. "The cunt!"

"You know him, don't you?"

"We went to the same weight-loss clinic. I pestered him until he told me how he'd lost all the weight, but that prick is a sly bastard, once he knew this shit worked, he fucking sold the idea to a fucking billionaire. That's the only way he managed to survive, to keep what he calls his *avatar*." Vince pauses and can't stop the guilt showing. "It's the only way I've been able to, too. But he, he could have helped your mum. He got her into this!"

More than a little vexed, Nicole kicks the chair out from behind her and stomps across the room. "So that's why that shit is going on out there? He's making money from this and there's going to be millions of those things everywhere?"

"You only know the half of — "

The front of a large, reinforced army truck smashes through Vince's kitchen window, ploughing into the table and cutting him off mid-sentence.

Chapter 51

The engine is still idling, the army truck is in tip-top condition.

Vince looks up at the cab and sees Henry leaning through the window, smiling down at him. "Oooh, bloody hell, that was a bit close, lol."

Vince stands and coughs up plaster dust.

"We need to go. Now," Henry says, "I've been trying to phone you."

There's other people in the cab; Vince cranes his neck to see Donna and Monique. "What the fucking hell are you doing, Henry?"

"I did try to call."

"Is that him?" A dusty Nicole climbs over the truck's bonnet. Vince nods. She lunges at Henry but Vince intervenes. There's no recognition on Henry's face as he grumbles, "What's her problem?"

"I'll tell you when we're inside." Vince waves him off and whispers to Nicole, "Look, babe, we need to see what he wants, he has the manpower and everything. If we're all going to get out of this alive, this knobhead has the resources to make that happen."

Nicole grimaces but follows Vince into the truck.

Chapter 52

It's a horror film outside.

There are bald-headed Glutters screaming in the streets as squidgy red babies forcibly birth themselves out of spontaneous places on their bodies.

"There's not even any pattern to it," the ever-glacial Donna says, staring through the windscreen at a young woman who is bent double retching a baby from her misshapen mouth. "You would have thought that all Feeder births would be the same, all Drinkers, Druggers, but no, they're entirely random."

"Donna's been studying the births, Vince," Henry says with his usual enthusiasm, swerving past an overturned ambulance and speeding the wrong way down a one-way street.

"Why are you here?" Vince says, holding Nicole's hand tightly.

"There's been a bit of a problem with Project Greenland."

"What's Project Greenland?" Nicole asks.

"You don't want to know."

"Saccharose has reduced our funding," Henry announces with a manic cackle.

Vince shuts his eyes and wishes it would all just stop. "What happened?"

"It's not my fault," Henry insists. "It's all these uncontrollable rogue avatars." He gestures out the window at a man who is face-down in the gutter with a purple thing prolapsing through the back of his trousers. "He wants them all put into medically-induced comas whilst we use the majority of the manpower capturing the rogue Glutters." He stops and acknowledges Nicole for a second. "Everything has gone tits-up. We liquidised all the Killers and fed them to the Feeders as a last meal. It's bullshit, man. Gone to the moon on a jet plane. It's all gone proper fucking pants-on-the-head balls-up-the-bumhole Jurassic Park, mate."

Vince frowns at a couple of Henry's obscure analogies but gets the gist. "So, what the fuck are you doing?"

"Going to find Saccharose," Henry grins, adjusting the steering wheel slightly so he can clip a man who's in the midst of what appears to be an ocular birth.

"What the fuck is Project Greenland?" Nicole asks again.

Vince sighs; everyone needs to be on the same page. "Did you ever watch *Battle Royale* or, more recently, *Squid Game*?"

"Nah man, I don't trust seafood and I hate wrestling."

"Okay, it's like this..."

Chapter 53

"So where is Saccharose?" Monique asks.

"Scotland."

All faces goldfish at Henry.

"How the hell are we going to get to Scotland?" Vince demands.

"Extremely fast." Henry floors the accelerator and the truck passes cleanly through the middle of a double-decker bus, and half a dozen of its passengers.

"What's in Scotland?"

"Haggis. Men in skirts. Bagpipes."

"Who thinks we should throw Henry from the truck?" Vince asks the women.

"Jeez," Henry tuts, "you never could take a joke. He's pretty much a fucking coward and wants to hide away until all the rogue avatars are loaded up before we launch Project Greenland again. Saccharose has a fallout shelter. Fully stocked for two hundred people for at least one hundred years."

Vince is quite surprised by that piece of news. "And he's told you where this is?"

"Totally, I have the address written down." Henry pats the left breast of his t-shirt.

Vince looks with mild apprehension and curses the day he ever met this feckless fuckwit. "In your shirt pocket?"

Henry laughs. "Don't be stupid. Do you really think I'm that stupid?"

"Yes. Yes, I do. Very much so."

Henry rips the collar of his t-shirt down and there is an address tattooed, upside-down, on his left breast.

"You're fucking nuts!".

Somehow, they make it out of town. Apart from the odd twenty car pile-up, which Henry casually skirts around, and the odd lunatic racing away from what they clearly think is a zombie outbreak, the motorway is relatively dead.

Vince almost dares to think it might be okay after all, when all hell falls from the sky.

The first few fragments shoot ahead of them like massive fireworks but then they can hear it coming.

"Ah, yeah," Vince begins, "there's something I should have told you about."

In the rear-view mirror he sees Frenzel's Comet like a missile in the sky above the road.

Henry hits the brakes as a ball of blinding red fire the size of a mountain rockets overhead and crashes on the horizon.

On impact with the ground, the earth begins to quake with such ferocity that despite the crash site being miles away, the aftershock cracks come zigzagging towards them immediately.

"Kinda reminds me of that bit in the first Superman film," Henry says, reminiscing as the fissures approach.

"REVERSE!" The four others scream.

Somehow, Henry manages to reverse the truck out of harm's way and they all take a breather.

The horizon is a supernatural glow of red, infected clouds; lightning ripples across the sky, illuminating something the size of a small country.

Henry folds his arms and looks at Vince with scolding disapproval. "And what the fuck was that?"

Chapter 54

They pull in at Shotley services and it's strangely deserted.

"Where the fuck is everyone?" Monique wonders aloud.

"The avatars will automatically head for the nearest source of whatever it is they're hungering for," Donna guesses.

They stand outside the truck at the petrol station whilst Henry fills it up. Nicole huddles against Vince as they stare at the horizon.

"Why aren't there more ordinary people leaving the towns?" she asks.

"There's avatars everywhere. Who knows what the fuck is going on? Who knows what damage that thing has caused?"

"We're going to have to head towards it," Henry says, and for once he's deadly serious. He nods to the shape in the distance. "This is like Godzilla."

No one argues with him; he is the one who has the details to the safe place, after all.

"We should get some food," says Vince, pointing to the service station.

Henry shows genuine concern now. "But, mate," he whispers, "it's a fucking service station, it's all gonna be junk."

Vince heads towards the single-storey building, Nicole joins him. He calls back over his shoulder, "I don't suppose you've got any weapons in that truck, have you?"

Henry walks ahead of the group through the automatic doors, his fists clenched and raised. "These are all the weapons we need, baby." He kisses the knuckles on each hand.

Vending machines are overturned and their contents litter the floor. Sounds of smashing plates and overturning chairs echo across a nearby food court.

"Don't go in there!"

From behind a coin-operated fire engine poke the shaven heads of a pair of McDonald's workers. The one who's just spoken is a heavy-set lad in his late teens.

"What's in there?" Vince asks.

The lad steps out, his grey uniform covered in blood. He's as white as a sheet. "A baby came out of me."

"It's okay, son." Vince says, trying to sound heroic.

"Faye's been hiding her twinner in the big wheelie bin out back for the last three days," the boy says, and beckons to the other worker who's still behind the fire engine.

Vince thinks that's quite smart, stashing your avatar in a bin at McDonald's where there's going to be a pretty heavy supply of leftover junk food to nosh on.

The other employee — he's expecting another poor soul who couldn't keep themselves in check when it came to eating — comes cautiously out from behind the kids' ride.

She's tiny, a size eight at the most, and doesn't look old enough to have left school let alone be working in McDonald's. She has a haunted look in her eyes.

"Umm, why did you do the ritual?" Nicole asks the question that was on Vince's lips.

"Because I was fed up with wanting to kill everyone."

"That's why you mustn't go in there," the lad whispers, "Faye 2 got out of the bin!"

Vince shoves Henry towards the food court. "After you, mate, you've got the weapons."

"It's cool." Henry strides forward with the nonchalant bravado of a cage-fighter. "I did a boxercise class once."

"We better look for weapons," Vince tells the rest of them, "we can't go all the way to Scotland without any food. If they kill Henry, someone has to cut his left tit off."

"I'll do that," Nicole volunteers.

There's fuck-all in the way of weaponry on the floor of the service station foyer, not even cool makeshift stuff like there would be if this was a film. The vending machines are intact, aside from being overturned and their fronts smashed into miniscule pieces. Donna and Monique peer around, clueless.

Henry opens the doors to the food court. "Come on, guys, I got you." Something red and wet *thwacks* against the glass and slides down the surface like a serial killer's chamois leather. There's an ear attached to it.

Henry pales. "Second thoughts, can we not just stop at the next services?"

Vince takes in Donna, Monique, Nicole, and the two Maccies workers. "We'll have to rush it. The Feeder shouldn't be a problem." Vince turns to the lad, "Look, there's no nice way to say this...I take it your double, your twinner, you had it removed because you're fat?"

The boy looks like he's about to cry, "I...I..." he pulls at his slightly constricting polo shirt, "I... I'm a gamer. My mum said I spent too much time playing on my PS6 and I needed to grow up and get a job."

"You're a fucking gamer!" Monique shouts.

"It's okay," Vince says, finding it ludicrous that someone would go through all that literal shit just to get rid of a game obsession. "And you're not fat." He addresses everyone, "Okay, so there's six of us and two avatars in there, a Killer, and a..." he shakes his head in disbelief, "...a Gamer. Fuck knows what the Gamer will be doing but we can guess what the Killer is or *has* been doing. Now, not all of you know this: the doubles can't be hurt, but they can be stopped, trapped. We need to go in there and grab the little bitch."

"Who are you calling a little bitch?" The Maccies worker seems to have reabsorbed some of that murderous lust.

Vince smiles awkwardly. "Let's go, on the count of...NOW!"

Anything to avoid further embarrassment, Vince uses his jogging experience to run full-pelt past the loitering Henry and into the food court. He hopes the others are following.

The food court is huge and there are bodies everywhere. A long-haired figure covered in blood stands on a table which is covered in leftover food and cardboard cartons.

It's the Killer.

She runs across the tabletops towards them.

Vince notices movement beneath the tables, there are still other customers hiding in there.

They use his distraction to crawl in the opposite direction.

Vince grabs the nearest chair and lobs it at the girl. It misses, but gives the others the idea to do the same.

She's getting closer, leaping from table to table without even faltering. Monique gets a lucky shot and one of the lightweight chairs clocks her full in the face and sends her flying. The girl somersaults backwards and falls under the tables.

She doesn't stop.

They hear further screaming as the Killer finds the retreating food court customers. Vince sees an elderly man get to his feet only to be dragged back down a second later by the girl who's part-zombie, part-wildcat.

Four other people make a break for it whilst she tears the old man to pieces.

They turn and run down the blood-slicked centre aisle.

"Fuck this shit," Vince cries, there's no fighting something that bloody quick, not without one of the guns the guys had at Project Greenland. "Let's get them out of here and try to trap it in the food court."

The girl jumps on two of the fleeing people's backs and claws out their throats. The last two customers try their best to run faster.

Vince ushers his crew out of the food court.

Henry stays put.

"Come on, you twat!"

Henry stands his ground, fists raised. "I can take her."

The two customers fly past Henry and he strikes out with a right jab to the Killer girl's face.

Vince is astonished to see the avatar slide across the floor unconscious. "How the fuck?"

Henry opens his hand and in between his fingers are the tranquilliser darts. He grins sheepishly, "I forgot the gun like a dopey mare."

Chapter 55

They load up on the few provisions they can salvage from the food court bloodbath after locking the sleeping Killer in a storeroom. Henry watches the two McDonald's workers and the two food court survivors carry boxes of sesame seed buns, cheese slices, and bottles of water towards the van. He makes the others hold back. "There's not enough room for all of us."

"We've got a fucking army truck, Henry," Vince scoffs.

Henry grits his teeth, "Trust me, there's no room."

"What's in the back of the lorry?"

Henry turns away and walks toward the four newcomers.

"Henry!" Vince calls after him.

"Vince!" It's Donna who has the guts to tell him. "He's brought our avatars along for the ride."

Vince feels sick. He looks at Monique for confirmation and she nods.

"I ain't getting back in that truck with any of them things," says Nicole, and stubbornly walks away.

"They're drugged and safe," insists Donna.

Henry is loading the boxes into the army vehicle's cab whilst at the same time gesturing to a half-full car park.

"He's expecting us to split up, isn't he?" Nicole asks anyone who's listening.

"We are not responsible for those people," Donna states. "We're pushing our luck hoping that fucking Saccharose will let anyone in other than bloody Henry as it is, but he's our only chance, and Saccharose is definitely not going to let two McDonald's workers inside his secret bunker."

"Why?"

"Because, Monique, they aren't exactly going to offer anything to mankind, are they? He probably has grandiose designs of repopulating the world, you know what these mega-rich people are like."

"What's wrong with McDonald's workers? They might have something to offer. And for all we know, the other two might be doctors."

"It doesn't matter, we can't save everyone." Donna walks over to join Henry and points out a Volkswagen camper van.

Vince takes hold of Monique's wrist just as she's about to follow her. "Why does he have our avatars, Monique?"

Monique is scared but she answers, "He said for insurance."

Vince lets her go.

He and Nicole watch as Donna breaks into the VW camper like an expert and gets it started up.

The two McDonald's workers get in the back and the older two get in the front. Henry leans into the driver's side and appears to give them directions. The van pulls off and vanishes down the slip road to the motorway.

Vince marches over to Henry and slams him against the truck. Henry's wild-eyed and panicked, flinching as if he's waiting to be punched.

"You've got our avatars!" Vince growls.

"It's not what you think, it's not what you think," Henry promises. "I've kept them safe since the Robert and Michael affair, to keep us safe."

"And to use as bribes."

Henry tries his best to feign innocence. "I hadn't even thought about that."

"Bullshit."

"In fact, you should be grateful," Henry snaps, pushing Vince away. "If it wasn't for me setting up the elite ward, your avatars would all be underground like the others and we all know what will happen if the meds wear off before I'm there to reload everything." He wags a finger at all of them. "Yeah. They'll start on the nearest food source - one another. Donna, you did a survey of the remaining avatars, didn't you?"

Donna nods in agreement.

"Tell them how many Feeders, Drinkers and Druggers we have."

"Over three thousand Drinkers, one thousand Druggers and," she pauses for effect, "fifteen thousand Feeders."

"And once those fuckers have eaten everything organic in the immediate vicinity, they will start on each other."

"So what?" Vince fails to see Henry's point.

"See? You're the true selfish bastard, Vince. You've only ever been in this to help yourself. What about Donna? What about Monique?" Henry glances guiltily at Nicole. "What about her?"

"I don't get you."

"The Feeders will take over. They will be the last ones standing. The only way you can get rid of an avatar is by completely eating the fucking thing and the Drinkers, Druggers and Killers and all the little one-offs aren't interested in consuming one another so eventually the only avs left will be the Feeders, especially now the ones with all the fight, the Killers, are obsolete. If they get out, we will have to face a world where there are unstoppable chomping machines eating us and everything else."

Vince sighs. "So, what's the fucking point?"

"I don't want to see that happen to these guys. I don't care what happens to those avatars back there. My friends won't go back to the way they were if they get consumed," Henry says, with such sincerity that Vince almost believes him.

"And I've got Aubrey Saccharose's avatar to bribe us all a place in the bunker."

"So, if he doesn't let us in whilst the illegal avatars are captured, you'll threaten to feed his rapist avatar to our two Feeders and turn him back into a rapey bastard underneath a mountain, or whatever, with whoever else he has under there?"

"Exactamundo, my dude!" Henry grins.

"Won't that take a long time? What if we've got a hundred rogue Feeders chasing us, trying to eat our arses for afters?"

"Oh, it's okay, Aubrey's avatar is in liquid form," Henry smiles triumphantly.

Donna raises her hand. "That was my idea."

Lost for words, Vince looks back at Henry.

"He's currently a thirty-litre smoothie in the back of that truck."

"You never fail to surprise me, Henry, do you know that?"

Henry takes that as a compliment.

Once they're back on the road, they go back to the plan of heading north, which unfortunately is the same direction as the seething red evil on the horizon.

Nicole finds a live news broadcast. She props her phone up on the dashboard so they can all at least get an idea of whatever it was that crash-landed a few hours earlier.

There's a newsreader wearing a hazmat suit, shouting into a microphone.

He's a professor of something.

Behind him is a war zone.

Soldiers are firing at a mass of writhing figures. It's unclear whether they are avatars or civilians.

In the distance, about two or three miles away, amidst the remnants of a freshly destroyed city or town, obscured by smoke, fires, further explosions, rises a wall of grey.

"There is reason to suspect the onslaught of what are being labelled *twinners*, is the result of the new Glutter cult. As yet, we can't confirm if these individuals who are rioting all over the country are the original cult members or, as has been suggested, doppelgangers birthed by the cult members after performing a separation ritual. We have shown the multiple births, but as yet, we haven't been able to examine any of the babies or mothers."

There's overhead footage of a town in ruins and a smouldering, flattened trail of destruction. The professor continues to talk over this segment.

"In reference to Frenzel's Comet, it appears to have changed trajectory as it was due to leave our skies and it gained abnormal speed and crashed into the centre of Edinbur —"

"Oh, for fuck's sake!" Henry screams, and punches the steering wheel.

"It appears that the comet was a vessel, or perhaps even a shell, for a gigantic alien entity. This is an amazing discovery, a truly wonderful day for science." The professor sounds excited. "Whilst the creature seems sentient, as yet it's been unresponsive, but we're going all-out to try to communicate with this visitor from the stars."

A helicopter flies over it and it's only from this height that they can see the grey wall isn't a wall but just a tiny bit of the thing from space.

It's humongous; Edinburgh Castle sits on its crag below it, and it's minute in comparison. The thing looks like someone spliced a blobfish with the most morbidly obese person they could find.

It slumps like a sleeping baby, this spherical splotch of gelatinous flesh. There is no neck at all. Its mouth bears a slight resemblance to Earth's basking shark in that it appears to be permanently open and lined with endless teeth. The mouth seems to occupy all of its head, or it is its head.

As the helicopter circles, it catches a shot of a rubbery antenna that dangles over what little face it has, it's reminiscent of an illicium, the angler fish's modified dorsal fin, except, as yet, the entity's doesn't appear to glow.

Four thick arms flop lazily on top of its ten-mile-wide belly.

Chapter 56

There's live footage of The Glut as it sits on Edinburgh. It's not doing anything.

"It looks dead," Henry says, after a quick scan of the phone screen.

"And how the hell would you know what it looks like when it's alive?" Nicole bites back.

"I've seen it before," Vince begins, "why am I the only one who remembers bloody well seeing it during the ritual?"

"You saw that thing during your ritual?" Donna says, with sudden animation.

"Yeah, I sort of passed out for a bit and I think I went to wherever it comes from, or what it travels on."

"So *that's* what you were going to tell us." Henry slows and steers around a wide crack in the road.

"I looked at the comet through a telescope and it all came back to me. It spoke in my head. I think we were connected for a moment."

"What's it doing, Vince?" Nicole leans into him, not daring to take her eyes from the phone.

"I don't know, but I doubt it's dead. I think it's waiting, or becoming acclimatised to our planet. It was much, much bigger when I saw it." Vince tries his best to mentally reach out to the thing on the screen, to find out what it wants.

"Let's just get to Saccharose's bunker and leave that fucking thing to the government. Only 110 miles to Edinburgh and none of us are wearing sunglasses." Henry puts his foot down, avoids the increasingly wider impact fissures, honks the horn at the occasional carful of survivors who have somehow managed to defy all odds and escape the doom-filled towns, although now and then, he runs some of them off the road.

"It's doing something."

Vince wakes up, wondering who spoke. Nicole's snoring against his shoulder, Henry is still driving, Donna and Monique are glaring at a phone.

Vince rubs the sleep away, leans over to see what's happening.

"They're trying to make contact." Donna tilts the screen so Vince can see.

The Chinook helicopter that flies towards the Glut's mouth is but a gnat in comparison, a dragonfly hovering over a volcano crater.

A series of lights and sounds come from something inside the chopper.

"Anyone who has watched any kind of sci-fi knows this shit isn't going to end well," Vince groans.

"They're going through the basic procedures for such an encounter," Donna whispers, as though the thing on the screen will hear her.

"What the hell did you do before this?"

"Government stuff, science stuff, bit of this, bit of that."

"Proper wheeler-dealer." Donna jumps in her seat. "Look! It's moving again!"

Vince sees the aerial thing on top of its head that he thought was a horn during his hallucination moves.

"It's like a gigantic, greasy, naked, Teletubby," Henry scowls in disgust. "Winky-Wanky's gone bye-bye, I'm telling you."

The Glut's grey protuberance twitches and begins to rise like a meaty crane. Vince expects the end of it to throb or glow like E.T's finger.

Something goes wrong with the Chinook: it loses power and falls inside the living volcano. On its way down, it clips one of the skyscraper teeth and splits in half before exploding.

Vince pushes the phone away. "Well, that went well and entirely as expected."

The news reporter is warbling on about the helicopter crash being a possible accident and that at the moment, there is no word on whether they are going to repeat the attempt at communication.

"Are they really this stupid?" Henry laughs. "How many choppers will they send into that thing's belly before they realise it doesn't want to be friends?"

"They're probably already trying to take samples from it whilst it seems to be asleep." Donna is still glued to the phone screen. "I think the antenna movement was involuntary, myself."

Vince is astonished at how cool she is being about this. "Henry, tell us about this book you found."

"Where I got the ritual from?"

"Yeah, Nicole told me all about it."

"How the hell did she know about it?"

"She was your girlfriend's daughter."

Henry slams on the brakes and stares at the sleeping woman. "Oh, shit."

"Yep."

"Fuck." There's actual emotion on Henry's face again. "I tried to help her, her mum, after we did the ritual, but we didn't know about the fucking birthing part of it. Nothing in the pages I saw said anything about the bloody avatars!"

"It's the age-old cliché," Vince sighs, "there's always a catch with shit like this. Always. Well, in the films, anyway."

Henry nods in agreement. "We couldn't afford to keep them constantly fed, but because we knew it worked, we had to find someone else to bring into it who could afford the aftermath."

"That's where Saccharose comes into it."

"Yeah, the dirty, filthy rapist pig," Henry says. "You think Jimmy Savile was bad, he had nothing on this guy."

"Jesus, and you helped him?"

"He genuinely wanted to stop the impulses before the allegations got so severe they couldn't be ignored and people couldn't be paid off."

"And what? You ran out of time and Nicole's mum got eaten by her avatar, and went back to square one?"

"Pretty much."

"What about the book? Where is it? Maybe there's something in it that can help us send The Glut back."

"No, it just tells you how to free yourself from its binds, nothing else." Henry slumps over the steering wheel and Vince almost feels sorry for him.

Thrashing sounds come from the back of the truck.

"It's reeling us in," Donna says. Her face lit by the only illumination in the vehicle, she shows them all her phone. "It's reeling us all in."

Chapter 57

The thing on The Glut's head waggles and winds like a giant's finger.

On the news screen, there are scores of newborn adolescent avatars on the crumbling streets of Edinburgh. They are not wandering aimlessly but walking with a purpose, heading towards their maker, their god. Their expressions cast the same emotionless vista as they have been doing since their birth but they've stopped doing what they were designed to do. They clog the roads and pathways; not one of them misses its footing, falls down any of the holes, or trips on any of the debris. Trailing amongst them are the avatars' hosts, the ones who expelled these monsters; they don't fare so well on their journeys.

They don't all look like doubles yet; most seem to be parents and teenage children.

The camera picks up an extraordinary moment when a haggard avatar leads its human double up a fractured street. The human, fear on his face, vanishes down a rent in the tarmac, and seconds, later the avatar ages and is instantly aware of its surroundings and the madness of it all.

It turns and flees in the opposite direction.

"Did you see that?" Donna is amazed. "Once you're reabsorbed, it has no hold over you."

"That's the only way out of this?" Nicole stares blankly through the glass.

"What the hell does it want?" Henry asks.

"To eat us all, by the looks of things." Monique begins to sob.

"It can't kill us," Vince suddenly laughs, "it can't. If it destroys mankind, then no one will feed it."

"I'm sure it will be fine without us."

"We feed it. Without us, it will starve."

"You're right," Nicole says, glaring at Henry, "*he* told my mum that there are other things outside our universe like that thing and they all made us and put a bit of themselves in the mix. Those pieces make us weak, make us do things that aren't always the best or healthiest thing to do and it feeds them, they get off on it. Grow on it."

"That's right," Henry admits.

The avatars are going ballistic in the back of the truck.

"They can't get out," Henry insists.

Monique lets out a hollow laugh and tears come. "So that's it, then? I have to go back to being a fucking smackhead again? I don't think I can live with that shit."

"My mum went and killed herself after she reabsorbed her double," Nicole says, before she realises it probably wasn't the best thing to say. "But you don't have to do that."

"Please," the ex-addict appeals to Henry and Vince, "there's got to be another way."

Donna wraps her arms around her, "It's okay, it will be okay. This time around, we're all in this together."

"I don't even think this thing is inherently evil. It's just here to put things back how they should be. To show us that we are powerless against it," Vince thinks aloud. "I definitely don't want to go back to the way I was, but the only way out of that either now or later is suicide and I'm not sure I wanna kill myself if that greasy fucker is a genuine glimpse of our afterlife."

"We're fucked either way, then," Henry hisses. "Shit, shit, shit."

There is nothing to do other than watch The Glut on the live news feed as it pulls everyone who betrayed its rules back to put things right. But there is nothing it can do about the avatars in the truck or sleeping within Project Greenland. The very air around The Glut is afloat with avatars and people. They climb and crawl up its sticky gelatinous skin like bugs. Everything is sucked into that never-ending mouth.

"Umm, Vince," Henry says, pointing to the screen, "I hate to state the obvious but he's eating everyone.

Maybe he's not going to put us all back together again. Maybe he's just going to eat us."

"But he'll starve."

"Mate, think about the population of Earth, yeah? The number of nutters that fell for this shit is probably nothing compared to the rest who don't even believe what they're seeing on live telly."

"Shit. Well, we'll have to make sure he doesn't get ours. If he starts eating everything, we're fucked either way. And I don't even think this is the actual Glut."

"You what?"

"When I saw him, he was bigger than you can imagine. Big enough to eat planets. I saw stars in his mouth. I think he's sent his avatar."

"Oh great, so not only is it the size of a fucking mountain, it's near enough indestructible. Yep, we're fucked." Henry leans back, resigned to his fate.

"Guys," Nicole whispers, "what happens if we eat it?"

Laughter explodes from both Henry and Vince.

"You can't eat a god!" Vince splutters, "and that thing is massive."

"No," Donna says, locking eyes with Nicole, "but fifteen thousand Feeders could."

"You. Are. Taking. The. Piss!" Vince coughs.

"They will naturally locate the nearest food source," Donna says, prodding Henry. "We need to turn this thing around and go back to Greenland."

"But the bunker!" Henry whines.

"I hate to say it, mate, but those things are loose back there," adds Vince. "Whatever the hell you've drugged our fuckers with, the Glut's pull is stronger. Also, our two fat bastards are in there, do you honestly think they're going to leave a thirty-litre Aubrey thickshake alone?"

"Saccharose!" Henry squeals — so do the brakes, when he slams his foot down hard.

Chapter 58

The closer they get to Edinburgh, the worse the road.

They all climb out of the truck and leave it to shake on its axles as the avatars try to break out.

"See, told you they wouldn't be able to get out," says Henry, smugly.

"So, what are we going to do?" Vince says, eyeing up a small case Henry procures from the cabin.

"Try and punch-tranq them again." Henry opens the case to show them it's full of tranquiliser darts.

"Mate, four adult avatars are going to come jumping out of there."

"Which is why you're going to help me." Henry slips six darts between the fingers of both hands.

Vince doesn't even begin to protest. "Fuck's sake." He copies Henry and after he has his darts, turns to Donna so she can remove the caps from the syringes.

"Right, Donna, Mon," Henry orders, "when I say 'go', open the doors and get back into the front of the truck as quickly as you can, okay?"

They nod.

"What about me?" Nicole asks.

"Just stand there looking tasty," Henry winks. Nicole gives him the finger.

"Ready?" Henry asks Vince.

"No, not at all. We're going to get torn apart."

"Go!" Henry shouts, crouching in a combat stance.

Donna and Monique both grab a handle, yank open the two doors and run.

A wave of chunky pink mulch slaps into Henry as though the truck has defied all logic and vomited on him. The torrent takes him by surprise, full in the face, and the force of it knocks him on his back. A figure jumps out behind the lumpy tsunami and pounces on him.

Donna's avatar drags herself across the bed of the truck, something is wrong with her legs. Henry's avatar barrels out over the top of her and Vince's immediate reaction is to turn and run. He's hardly made any distance before he wrings his ankle like a horror movie cliché and rolls onto his back.

Henry's avatar isn't so clumsy, it heads straight for him.

"Hey!" Vince can hear Nicole trying to get the avatar's attention but he's only interested in the nearest food. Vince puts his hands over his head and cowers and the avatar drops on top of him.

Within seconds, it goes limp.

The tranquillisers.

Vince lets the avatar roll off him, gets up, and tries his best to make it seem like he planned for the attack to happen that way.

Henry's covered in pink, and Vince's avatar has him pinned down; whilst he licks the gunk off him, the tranquilliser darts are scattered across the road. Donna and Monique try to pull the avatar off him but he's too strong and Donna's avatar has flopped from the truck and wrapped his arms around Monique's ankles.

The skinny woman hits the ground and her attacker bites down on her exposed hamstring.

Nicole ferrets amongst the truck slush and finds Henry's dropped darts. She jams one into the opened mouth of Donna's avatar just as she's about to chomp down into Monique's leg again. She crunches the syringe and its contents lazily for a few seconds and then slumps forward.

Vince kicks his own avatar in the face and screams at the pain that lances up his leg. His avatar is pushed back for a few seconds but it's long enough for Henry to find one of the darts and stick it up under his chin.

Henry scoots backwards on his hands and feet whilst Vince's avatar crumbles.

Back on the truck, something in the shadows twitches and reaches for the fresh air.

Monique's avatar.

They gather round and see she's had the majority of her guts torn out by the two Feeders. She's barely intact, just held together by her spinal column.

"Fuuuuuuuuck," groans Henry.

Monique sees her avatar and starts to slip into the hyperventilating throes of an anxiety attack.

"Gimme," Nicole says, taking a dart from Vince and hopping up into the truck, batting away feebly protesting hands and sinking the tranquilliser home.

Chapter 59

"What are we going to do about Saccharose?" Henry wails, stomping his feet like a spoiled toddler. His chance of bribing the billionaire rapist slides along the road like a sentient blancmange.

"Henry, there are more important things to worry about," Donna snaps. There are three comatose avatars on the tarmac and one in the back of the truck and Monique is bleeding from a deep, gushing leg wound.

"First-aid kit in the glove box," he waves her words away and continues to look longingly as the Saccharose smoothie slips away.

Vince and Nicole get Monique into the truck whilst Donna raids the glove compartment for bandages before preparing to store the avatars.

The rear of the vehicle is clear of the Saccharose smoothie but it's an explosion of medical apparatus. They cobble together what they can to bind the two Feeders before assessing the damage done to Monique and Donna's avatars.

Monique's avatar is virtually in two pieces, but when Henry examines the ragged wound edges, they're already healing rapidly. It'll take a few days but there's no reason why she won't regenerate after he's hooked her back up to the intravenous drip.

Donna's avatar has had most of the meat eaten from the knees down, any more and the double of the ex-alcoholic really would be legless. They hook her back up to her gin drip and Henry pumps them with all the sedatives he's got.

With a sullen expression, Henry slumps back behind the wheel. "Let's go back to Project Greenland, then, and hope this fucking stupid plan works." Still swearing, he turns the lorry in a U-turn and heads back the way they came from.

Chapter 60

"I'm not feeling too well," Monique says, right before a wet squelch and the most pungent of smells floods the cabin.

Nicole retches, leans across Vince, and unwinds the window as quickly as possible.

Monique is slouched in her seat, a sheen of sweat slickening her skin. A fan of vomit sprays over her chest. "Oh, for fuck's sake."

"She's going through withdrawal," Donna says, and searches for something in the glove box for her to be sick in.

"Oh, for Jesus-ing sake." Henry's driving one-handed, a sleeve held across his mouth and nose. "Can we put her in the back?"

"Pull over," Donna shouts. Henry does as he's told.

"Vince, swap with Mon so she can sit by the window," Donna orders.

"But I don't want to have to sit in the wet patch."

"Either that, or you're in the back."

"Ah, for fuck's sake."

After the change around, Monique half-hangs out of the window; every few miles, she vomits into the night.

"We need to stop off at my house," Nicole tells them. "If I'm in this too, then we're getting my avatar."

"Bloody great," Henry grunts. "How many darts have we got left?"

Vince looks. "Two."

"Wonderful."

"How big is your avatar?" Henry says, drudgingly.

"She's exactly the same as me: size, shape, and everything."

"Really?" Vince purrs with a lecherous grin.

Nicole shoots him a look that seems to zap through the centre of his eyeballs and ricochet around the inside of his skull, blitzing all dirty thoughts in a single heartbeat.

"Right, okay. Let's get the bitch," Henry shrugs. "You'd better have something to restrain her, though."

Chapter 61

"This just in.

"The site surrounding the entity has been evacuated. As you can see by our footage, the steady influx of twinners has dwindled to a trickle. Numerous attempts have been made to make contact with the entity but not only is it proving to be hostile, see the earlier Chinook footage, but it also seems to be secreting toxins unknown to mankind that may or may not be harmful. Unfortunately it has been decided to destroy the entity in case it decides to relocate and cause more damage."

"They're going to kill it?" Vince can't believe what he's hearing. They've been driving in silence for an hour or so, Monique has puked herself dry and is like a furnace to the touch. Donna has noticed mild withdrawal symptoms but nothing she can't handle.

"Yeah," Nicole squeaks, "wanna see?"

"They're going to do it now?" He is surprised the news would televise such a thing and really must remember to commend the BBC for such a wonderful and convenient service of a quasi-apocalyptical event.

Henry pulls over so they can all watch The Glut hopefully be destroyed and save them all a lot of hassle.

The camera footage has changed, it's gone all hi-tech, night visiony and military. The Glut is a big black clump with a huge white cave for a mouth. Two fighter jets fly over it once from left to right and then a pair of black rockets fall down into that Brobdingnagian chasm.

Nothing happens at first.

Then...nothing happens.

Then, all of a sudden...more nothing.

Henry clears his throat. "So, how long do you reckon those things take to go off?"

Something happens.

"Okay, that's probably not a good thing," Vince moans as the Glut's four thick arms twitch into movement and it pushes itself up off of Edinburgh.

It stands up on a pair of short elephantine stumps.

They hear it move a hundred miles away.

The Glut tramples over the ruined city; a mega-ton arm swats in the direction of the military camera, and there's no more footage.

"Oh lord, he's coming," Henry says as the ground begins to shake.

"I don't want you to think bad of me," Nicole whispers to Vince as Henry speeds like fuck to her house.

"Why would I?"

"My avatar isn't exactly kept in…" she searches for the appropriate word, "…umm, humane conditions."

Vince laughs, "Babe, you've not seen Project Greenland."

"But this all shows us the shit we're capable of when we discover something that's a little less than human."

Vince doesn't know what to say to that.

Her house is nice, what they see of it from the outside. Nicole shows Vince round to the back garden, where there's a covered outside pool.

"Whoa, my girlfriend has a swimming pool!"

"Yeah, you might not want to swim in it after you see what's in there." Nicole unfastens the tarpaulin and the stench hits him.

"You keep her in there?"

Nicole pulls back the tarpaulin and reveals what's inside.

Her avatar looks like a victim of the worst kind of abuse.

There isn't a millimetre of unblemished, untainted skin.

She's a human slug.

Heavy chains are wound around and threaded between her arms and legs in such a way that she's only able to flop like a seal. The chains are filthy, encrusted with dried shit and vomit and rusted by being steeped constantly in piss and blood. She's in a worse state than the chains and it's truly a godsend that the avatar can't feel pain: the chains dig into her flesh where it's even healed over in places. Her hair hangs in thick, matted clumps, her teeth are brown stumps that get in the way as she wriggles and writhes back and forth along the pool bottom, licking, puking, pissing, and shitting without any break.

Vince gawks at the avatar until Nicole's sobbing brings him out of it. "Ummm, have you got a hose?"

Together, they haul Nicole's avatar from the pool and as they cross her garden, they can hear the army truck starting up. For a second, Vince thinks Henry is going to leave them in the lurch, but then the ground begins to shake and they know The Glut is gaining on them. There's no time to worry about sedating Nicole's avatar. They throw her in the back of the truck, get in, and drive like fuck towards Project Greenland.

"I can see it!" Henry shrieks, a high-pitched falsetto that would make the Bee Gees envious. Behind them in the distance, the horizon is filled up with the colossal, rotund figure of the Glut, its silhouette is like a four-armed cartoon ghost. Steering becomes more difficult the closer it gets.

They're on the outskirts of the town where Project Greenland is hidden. Henry heads straight for the closed multi-storey car park. "How long is it going to take to wake them all up?" asks Vince.

Henry looks as if he's just been slapped. "The system feeds them all simultaneously, if I stop it, about half an hour."

Vince winces.

"Shit and fuck."

"What are we going to do, Henry? You fucking got us all into this shit!"

They stop by the car park; Henry's knuckles are white as he grips the steering wheel and tries not to cry. "Okay, can you drive?"

"No," Vince says.

"I can," offers Nicole.

"Drive around...ummm...distract it...when you see the car park lit up like Christmas, come as quick as you can." Henry gets out of the truck.

"You're going down underground whilst we're up here with that fucking thing?"

"Yes, Vince, with fifteen thousand pissed-off, hungry Feeders."

"I'll come with you. You'll need help with the meds." Donna gets out and joins Henry. Monique murmurs unintelligibly in the corner.

"Once you get back here, we'll get back in and get out of here, so be ready," Henry barks. He and Donna disappear.

Nicole scoots over into the driving seat. "I have no idea where I'm going."

A thunderous noise breaks through the night: guttural, with the vaguest aspects of something ornithological but demonically alien and entirely hostile.

Chapter 62

The buildings shake as The Glut storms towards the town.

"What the fuck do I do, Vince?" shouts Nicole.

Vince leans over the comatose Monique and out of the window, it's the only way he can get a look at The Glut in its entirety.

It's the size of a mountain. There's still no telling how far away it is due to its sheer size.

He scans the darkened horizon near its feet and finally sees several tower blocks brushed aside like Lego bricks.

"Drive faster," he yells, "just keep going straight. It's about a mile away." If it had any sense, or the flexibility, even, it could bend down and pick them up. The downsize to The Glut is that it wasn't designed to be mobile. It was a thing that spent its existence immobile, in a continuous state of consumption.

The air smells of hot, rancid, rotten fat; Vince remembers the newscaster saying something about it possibly being toxic. He slides back in and yanks up the window.

The Glut lets rip one of those abnormal roars again and something thick and mucoid flies over the truck and lands with a splat and a steaming sizzle in the road ahead.

The headlights pick it up, a mass of creamy, stringy yellow, heaving with mangled, part-digested, but moving, avatar parts.

Nicole swerves to avoid it but the clump springs at the truck like a gelatinous spider made of custard.

Arms and feet pound at the windscreen. The skin sloughs off, pizza topping aided by The Glut's digestive juices, spreading tacky slime across the glass and obscuring their vision.

A barrage of disembodied penises and vaginas slap against the passenger window; everything has been semi-dissolved, half-absorbed in The Glut's infernal gut and its sentient puke begins to seep through the edges of the glass.

"I can't see where the fuck I'm going!" Nicole screams.

Vince ducks as the window disintegrates and the dicks and cunts attach to Monique like suckers and hoist her from the seat and out of the truck. One second, she's there, the next she's gone, not a peep out of her.

"Monique," Vince goldfishes, but Nicole's too busy being distracted by other things.

The sicktopus glissades over the front of the truck as a windscreen wiper burns away in the acidic bile. The truck bumps up and crashes through something hard but it's military issue and made for tougher shit than this.

The omelette of semi-solid bits and bobs scrapes away from his side and Vince can see they're in an abandoned supermarket. Empty shelves rocket past. "Crash into stuff more."

"What?"

"Crash into stuff more, try and shake this shit off us!"

Nicole doesn't even have to try to do that. It's as though objects purposefully jump into her path, mannequins, boxes, display units, but it takes a whole tobacco kiosk to knock the fucking thing off them. She lets out a triumphant whoop as her view is suddenly clear. Ahead there's a wall of shuttered glass: she slams her foot down on the accelerator and steers in that direction.

The Glut gives another of its unearthly shrieks and as they burst from the dead supermarket, a foot as wide as a tornado flattens the building and they're driving between its legs. It's raining yellow fat down on them and the ground is thundering as it moves its clumsily epic body to try and stomp their puny vehicle.

They can't go fast enough, its strides are half a mile long; as Henry says, it's all gone Jurassic Park.

Nicole twists and turns the steering wheel, and the avatars break through the fugue of sedation and start screaming in the rear. Meanwhile, Vince cries like a six-year-old boy who's just caught a cricket ball in the bollocks. The Glut's frustrated roars deafen, and just as they think it's all over, floodlights brighter than the sun almost blind them.

"Greenland!" they shout, and Nicole narrowly avoids them getting squashed by one of The Glut's feet and drives through anything to get to those lights.

Vince can hear the avatars kicking at the truck doors and he hopes to hell they won't break free. To get this far only to fail would be just typical.

Project Greenland is up ahead and they know they have to stop for Henry and Donna—and this is where Nicole fucks up.

She tries to do one of those cool handbrake turns as she's no doubt seen stuntmen do in the films, but manages only to flip the truck onto its side. Henry and Donna stare in utter defeat as it rolls through the air towards them.

Chapter 63

All around come the sounds of human and alien screaming.

The army truck is upside down, Vince hurts everywhere, but he thinks he and Nicole are okay for the moment. He unclips their seat belts and they fall onto the roof. He crawls out of the passenger window and can see they've made it into the ground floor of the multi-storey car park.

The back of the truck has burst open; Henry is wrestling with his avatar, who has just escaped.

Donna has her arms hooked around one of the legs of hers and it's dragging her along.

As soon as they see their avatars, Vince and Nicole dash for them to prevent their escape.

Vince rugby-tackles his and it squirms beneath him like an oversized unruly toddler. Nicole is lucky, her avatar is still chained up.

A terrific crash resounds all around and the top of the car park is torn away.

The Glut towers over them.

It roars, its four arms extended downwards, dripping burning fat onto them.

The proboscis on its head vibrates and the four avatars begin to lift off the ground as though in holy rapture. Monique's is already gone, a speck on its way to The Glut's eternal maw.

Henry, Donna, Vince, and Nicole cling to their suddenly docile avatars as though their lives depend on it.

"Where are the Feeders?" Vince screams to Henry as they're being dragged along across the car park beneath their floating doubles.

"I had to set a timer on the doors so we could get out," he screams, using every bit of energy to hold on to his avatar's ankles.

Donna's the first one to leave the ground and she never lets go, not even when they see her fly up and vanish into The Glut's ever-open grin.

An explosion stuns them, even the gigantic behemoth above, and the avatars dip a little in their levitation, enabling Vince and the others to gain more purchase.

The swarm of Feeders storms over and around them as an overpowering reek of animal stench, body odour, faecal matter and rot takes them to The Glut's legs, where they attack and climb.

The Glut's antenna is a blur; a few of the Feeders start to bob in the air but the majority still pillage its lower legs of all substance.

Henry, Vince and Nicole's avatars are still completely enthralled and they're finding it harder to hold on.

Vince sees the struggle on Henry's face as he puts every muscle in his body under extreme pressure to hold on to the part of him that he expelled. *It's not worth it.* "Let go, Henry! It's gonna take us with it."

"It's going to take us with it anyway!"

Vince can feel his avatar sliding from his grasp. He doesn't think so. He still thinks The Glut is only here to set things right. "Ah, fuck it," he says and lets go. He falls back and his avatar flies up into the air.

"Vince, no!" Nicole shouts.

He knows neither of them will make the same decision and he can't force them to. He stands, and just as he suspects, he isn't whisked up into the air.

A large part of him wants to run as far away as he can before his avatar is reabsorbed but he pounces on both Henry and Nicole and offers his strength to help them hold on to their embodied weaknesses.

The noise The Glut makes as it falls to one knee is like all the babies of the world crying at once.

The Feeders infest its upper body.

They see its black eyes, too small for such a colossus, glow red, and in the heavens above, a red star glows.

"Let go, Vince," Henry says, "I can't hold on any longer."

"No," Vince pleads, "We can do this. We're not on our own anymore. We can do this the proper way. Together."

"I'd rather die than be like that again for even one second," Henry smiles sadly, then bites down hard on Vince's arm.

Vince recoils and silently watches Henry and his avatar disappear up into the void.

Red lightning fills the skies as the red star pulsates and bleeds onto The Glut.

The Feeders are crawling all over it, ants on a carcass, they are covered head-to-toe in its greasy secretions, tunnelling in and out of its fattened arteries, eating their fill.

The Glut increases its pull over them and a high percentage of the fat-miners get consumed through its pores.

Nicole stubbornly clings on to her avatar's slippery calves; Vince will support her to the end.

The Glut bellows with rage as it too starts to lift from the ground. The red star, which Vince assumes is the genuine Glut and not just this smaller avatar, calls it back.

Its job is almost done.

"You promise you'll never, ever give up and let go?" Nicole stammers, her fingers sliding over slick skin.

"I promise."

Nicole shuts her eyes and says goodbye to her avatar.

Vince and Nicole fall to the ground and the red star explodes, lighting up the sky.

The Glut, its skin infested with avatars, is sucked into a bleeding crimson hole.

Epilogue: A Lesson For All Mankind

The glut had a strong hold over humanity even after this story ends but mankind is now aware, although some still seriously doubt, of its existence.

Although Vince and Nicole reabsorbed their avatars they also absorbed each other, they discovered that together they had enough willpower for three people.

The same goes for mankind in general.

Many rise above their addictions, some fall,

It takes time but they don't give up and it helps knowing what they're fighting against.

They have each other.

They know there is no way to permanently rid themselves of their inner demons but with enough love, support and self-belief, they can keep them at bay.

Author Biography

Matthew Cash, or Matty-Bob Cash as he is known to most, was born and raised in Suffolk, which is the setting for his debut novel *Pinprick*. He is compiler and editor of *Death by Chocolate*, a chocoholic horror Anthology and the *12Days: STOCKING FILLERS* Anthology. In 2016 he launched his own publishing house Burdizzo Books and took shit-hot editor and author Em Dehaney on board to keep him in shape and together they brought into existence *SPARKS*: an electrical horror anthology, *The Reverend Burdizzo's Hymn Book, Under the Weather* * *Visions from the Void* ** and *The Burdizzo Mix Tape Vol. 1.*
He has numerous solo releases on Kindle and several collections in paperback.
Originally with Burdizzo Books, the intention was to compile charity anthologies a few times a year but his creation has grown into something so much more powerful *insert mad laughter here*. He is currently working on numerous projects; his third novel *FUR* was launched in 2018.
*With *Back Road Books*
** With Jonathan Butcher

He has always written stories since he first learnt to write and most, although not all, tend to slip into the many-layered murky depths of the Horror genre.
His influences ranged from when he first started reading to Present day are, to name but a small select few; Roald Dahl, James Herbert, Clive Barker, Stephen King, Stephen Laws, and more recently he enjoys Adam Nevill, F.R Tallis, Michael Bray, Gary Fry, William Meikle and Iain Rob Wright (who featured Matty-Bob in his famous *A-Z of Horror* title *M is For Matty-Bob*, plus Matthew wrote his own version of events which was included as a bonus).
He is a father-of-two, a husband-of-one, and a zookeeper of numerous fur babies.

You can find him here:
www.facebook.com/pinprickbymatthewcash

https://www.amazon.co.uk/-/e/B010MQTWKK

Other Releases by Matthew Cash

Novels

Virgin and the Hunter
Pinprick
Fur

Novellas

Ankle Biters
KrackerJack
Illness
Hell, and Sebastian
Waiting For Godfrey
Deadbeard
The Cat Came Back
KrackerJack 2
Werwolf
Frosty
Keida-in-the-Flames
Tesco agogo
Your Frightful Spirit Stayed

Short Stories

Why Can't I Be You?
Slugs and Snails and Puppydog Tails
Oldtimers
Hunt The C*nt
Clinton Reed's FAT

Anthologies Compiled and Edited by Matthew Cash & Em Dehaney

Death by Chocolate
12 Days: STOCKING FILLERS
12 Days: 2016 Anthology
12 Days: 2017
The Reverend Burdizzo's Hymn Book

Sparks
VISIONS FROM THE VOID (with Jonathan Butcher)
Under the Weather (with Back Road Books)

Anthologies Featuring Matthew Cash
Rejected For Content 3: Vicious Vengeance
JEApers Creepers
Full Moon Slaughter
Full Moon Slaughter 2
Freaks
No Place Like Home: Twisted Tales from the Yellow Brick Road
Down The Rabbit Hole: Tales of Insanity

Collections
The Cash Compendium Volume 1
The Cash Compendium Continuity

Website: www.Facebook.com/pinprickbymatthewcash

Printed in Great Britain
by Amazon